Trouble at Coyote Canyon

The wheels of the green jeep spun as the driver sped off, throwing up streams of dust and pebbles.

Frank dashed over to his horse, Star, jumped onto the saddle, and urged him into a gallop. As he closed in on the jeep, Frank heard more hoofbeats behind him and knew it was Joe. "You go left, I'll go right!" Joe shouted.

As Frank caught up to the jeep he freed his boots from the stirrups and used his knee and reins to bring Star as close as possible to the side of the vehicle. Then, gathering his strength, he leaped out of the saddle and into the backseat of the vehicle.

Frank was forced to duck when the driver made a blind swing with a metal tool. Frank scrambled behind the driver's seat, grabbed both of the guy's ears, and twisted them hard.

"Hit the brakes!" Frank shouted over the man's angry cries. "Right now!"

The Hardy Boys Mystery Stories

#59	Night of the Werewolf	#92	The Shadow Killers
#60	Mystery of the Samurai Sword	#93	The Serpent's Tooth Mystery
#61	The Pentagon Spy		
#62	The Apeman's Secret	#94	Breakdown in Axeblade
#63	The Mummy Case	#95	Danger on the Air
#64	Mystery of Smugglers Cove	#96	Wipeout
#65	The Stone Idol	#97	Cast of Criminals
#66	The Vanishing Thieves	#98	Spark of Suspicion
#67	The Outlaw's Silver	#99	Dungeon of Doom
#68	Deadly Chase	#100	The Secret of the Island Treasure
#69	The Four-headed Dragon		
#70	The Infinity Clue	#101	The Money Hunt
#71	Track of the Zombie	#102	Terminal Shock
#72	The Voodoo Plot	#103	The Million-Dollar Nightmare
#73	The Billion Dollar Ransom		
#74	Tic-Tac-Terror	#104	Tricks of the Trade
#75	Trapped at Sea	#105	The Smoke Screen Mystery
#76	Game Plan for Disaster	#106	Attack of the Video Villains
#77	The Crimson Flame	#107	Panic on Gull Island
#78	Cave-in!	#108	Fear on Wheels
#79	Sky Sabotage	#109	The Prime-Time Crime
#80	The Roaring River Mystery	#110	The Secret of Sigma Seven
#81	The Demon's Den	#111	Three-Ring Terror
#82	The Blackwing Puzzle	#112	The Demolition Mission
#83	The Swamp Monster	#113	Radical Moves
#84	Revenge of the Desert Phantom	#114	The Case of the Counterfeit Criminals
#85	The Skyfire Puzzle	#115	Sabotage at Sports City
#86	The Mystery of the Silver Star	#116	Rock 'n' Roll Renegades
#87	Program for Destruction	#117	The Baseball Card Conspiracy
#88	Tricky Business		
#89	The Sky Blue Frame	#118	Danger in the Fourth Dimension
#90	Danger on the Diamond		
#91	Shield of Fear	#119	Trouble at Coyote Canyon

Available from MINSTREL Books

119

The HARDY BOYS®

TROUBLE AT COYOTE CANYON

FRANKLIN W. DIXON

A MINSTREL® BOOK

PUBLISHED BY POCKET BOOKS

New York   London   Toronto   Sydney   Tokyo   Singapore

This book is a work of fiction. Names, characters, places, and incidents are either the product of the author's imagination or are used fictitiously. Any resemblance to actual events or locales or persons, living or dead, is entirely coincidental.

A MINSTREL PAPERBACK *ORIGINAL*

 A Minstrel Book published by
POCKET BOOKS, a division of Simon & Schuster Inc.
1230 Avenue of the Americas, New York, NY 10020

Copyright © 1993 by Simon & Schuster Inc.
Front cover illustration by Daniel Horne

Produced by Mega-Books of New York, Inc.

ISBN: 0-671-79309-8

First Minstrel Books printing April 1993

10 9 8 7 6 5 4 3 2 1

Printed in the U.S.A.

Contents

1. *The Wild West*   1
2. *Howls in the Night*   9
3. *Four-Legged Terror*   21
4. *Another Deadly Ride*   34
5. *The Figure on the Hill*   44
6. *Ambushed!*   54
7. *A Traitor in the Midst*   62
8. *Out of Control*   74
9. *Sniper Attack*   84
10. *Running Dry*   94
11. *A Saboteur Is Exposed*   102
12. *The Anasazi Connection*   110
13. *Missing Evidence*   120
14. *Stampede!*   128
15. *Into the Sunset*   134

TROUBLE AT
COYOTE CANYON

1 The Wild West

"Frank," Joe Hardy said excitedly, "you've got to catch this view." Seventeen-year-old Joe leaned closer to the window of the small commuter plane. "It's incredible—mountains as far as I can see. Some still have snow on them."

"All I can see is the back of your head," his older brother, Frank, said. He craned forward to glimpse the scenery through the window next to Joe's. It was every bit as spectacular as Joe had said.

"Is that where we're headed?" Joe asked. "It looks pretty rugged for a week-long tour on horseback."

The plane banked, giving Frank a look at the position of the afternoon sun. "Those mountains must be north of Durango," he said. "From what Mike Preston told us, we'll be heading west, into the mesa

1

country. That's pretty rugged, too, but different from the High Rockies."

Joe turned around, brushed back his blond hair, and winced. "Ow," he said, rubbing the back of his neck. "I gave myself a crick from looking out the window so long."

"That's what you get for hogging the view," Frank said. "I hope we can help Mike with his problem. But even if we can't, a wilderness trail ride will be quite a change from hanging around Bayport."

"I'm looking forward to meeting Mike," Joe said. "Why don't you fill me in some more? You only gave me a few details before we left."

Frank, who had dark hair and was a year older than his brother, shrugged his broad shoulders and stretched his legs. The rows of seats in the plane were a bit too close together for six-footers like him and Joe.

"There's not all that much to tell," Frank said. "Mike heads up an outfit called Teen Trails West, out in western Colorado. He got our names from Doug Newman, the windsurfer. Apparently they're old friends. Mike told Doug about the problems he's been having, and Doug suggested he call us. Doug told him we'd been a big help to him that time in France."

Joe nodded. He and Frank were well-known in their hometown, and beyond, as detectives. They had solved many difficult cases together, including Doug's.

"What kind of guy is Mike?" Joe asked.

Frank grinned. "Well, he looks like a cowboy—tall and skinny, about twenty-five, with shaggy brown hair, a dark tan, and—"

"I don't mean his appearance," Joe interrupted. "What was he *like?*"

"Worried," Frank replied. "He said he's put everything he has into Teen Trails West, and if it goes down the drain . . . Then he showed me this newspaper clipping."

Frank reached into his bag and pulled out a photocopy of a tabloid newspaper—the kind usually sold at supermarket checkout counters—and handed it to Joe. Joe had seen it before, but he scanned it again. The headline read, Talk Show Host's Daughter Encounters Horror on Horseback!

Just under it was a picture of a smug-looking dark-haired girl with scratches on her face and her wrist wrapped in bandages. The caption, in letters almost as big as the headline, read, Lorna Bradley: Teen Tour Terror Scarred Me for Life!

"She doesn't look that bad off," Joe remarked. "What really happened to her?"

"According to Mike, Lorna's horse got spooked and bucked her off," Frank said. "She landed in a mesquite bush, sprained her wrist, and got some pretty bad scratches on her face and arms."

"That doesn't sound much like 'scarred for life,'" Joe pointed out. "I can see that this kind of publicity is bad for Mike, but what does he want us to do for him? We're detectives, not public relations experts."

3

"Apparently Lorna's accident wasn't the only one they've had this summer," Frank replied. "*If* they're accidents. Mike doesn't think they are. He thinks somebody's out to ruin him. An operation like Teen Trails West depends a lot on word of mouth, and once it starts getting around that there are problems, people start canceling. Unless we can find out who's behind the sabotage, Mike doesn't know if he can even finish out the season."

The plane's loudspeaker came to life in a burst of static. "Ladies and gentlemen," the cabin attendant said, "we're beginning our approach to La Plata Airport, serving Durango, Colorado, and Mesa Verde National Park. Please be sure your seat belts are fastened, and thank you for flying with us today."

Frank spotted Mike Preston as soon as he and his brother entered the terminal. He was standing near the snack bar, holding up a sign that said Teen Trails West. He was dressed in faded jeans with a leather belt, fancy cowboy boots, and a plaid western shirt.

Next to Mike was a boy of about fourteen, with straight brown hair that flopped over one eye. He was wearing a black T-shirt with a big picture on it of a bright green praying mantis and the caption Bugs Are People, Too.

"Hi, guys," Mike called, waving. "How was your trip?"

"Great," Joe replied. He introduced himself to Mike, and the two shook hands.

"This is Nick Millhiser, from New York City," Mike

4

continued. "He's on this tour, too. Nick, meet Frank and Joe Hardy. They live right outside New York."

"I saw you on the plane," Frank said with a friendly smile. "Is this your first time at something like this?"

"It sure is," Nick said, sounding at once nervous and excited. "I've never been west of Pittsburgh before. It's really different here. And I like horseback riding, but I don't know about a whole week in the saddle."

Mike patted him on the back. "You'll do fine. We'll head for the car in a minute, but I'm expecting one more rider. I reckon that's her."

Frank and Joe followed Mike's glance. About twenty feet away, a girl was standing with her back to them. Her blond hair was done up in a complicated braid, and she was wearing a purple striped miniskirt over yellow tights, and an embroidered sleeveless vest.

Mike went over to her. Frank, Joe, and Nick trailed after him.

"Jessica Springer?" Mike said. "Hi, I'm Mike Preston. Didn't you see my sign?"

Jessica gave him a bored glance. "I didn't look," she drawled. "I knew somebody was meeting me, so I figured they'd, like, find me. There's my bag," she added, pointing to a tan leather suitcase with the initials of a famous fashion designer on it.

"Fine," Mike said cheerfully. "Bring it along. The car's outside." He turned and started toward the exit.

Jessica shot an angry look at his back, then aimed it at Frank and the two others as well. After a long pause, she bent down and picked up the suitcase. As the group followed Mike, Joe looked over at Frank and rolled his eyes.

Mike's car was a dusty jeep station wagon with a row of off-road driving lights mounted on the front of the roof rack. He opened the tailgate and stowed their bags, then headed for the driver's side.

"Hop in," he called.

Jessica had already settled herself in the other bucket seat in front, leaving Joe, Frank, and Nick to wedge themselves into the backseat. It was a tight fit.

As they pulled out of the parking lot, Jessica said, "We keep an old car just like this at our place up in the Sierras. My daddy says he'd be a fool to take any of the Mercedeses on those roads."

After a short, heavy silence, Mike said, "Jessica's from California—Beverly Hills. Her dad directs movies."

"Yeah? Neat," Nick said. "What did he do? Maybe I've seen one of them."

Jessica named three movies. Frank recognized two as big hits.

"Neat," Nick said again. "I know a girl at school whose brother was in a movie."

"Practically everybody I know has been in a movie," Jessica retorted. "I've been in two of them."

Frank glanced at Joe, who once again rolled his eyes.

"We're coming into Durango now," Mike said, breaking the new silence. "We don't have time to look around this afternoon, but maybe we will at the end of the tour."

"Are we heading for your ranch now?" Frank asked.

"That's right," Mike replied. He picked up speed as they left the town behind. "It's about twenty-five miles from here, east of Mesa Verde National Park."

Frank enjoyed looking at the scenery from the jeep. On the right were ranks of steep mountains, dark with evergreens. On the left, grasslands rolled toward a horizon broken by the jagged shapes of the purple mesas.

The trip from New York to Denver and then to Durango, together with the time difference, had tired Frank more than he realized. He closed his eyes for a moment. A minute later—or so it seemed—he was jolted awake.

"Look, Frank!" Joe was saying excitedly. "Coyotes!"

Frank opened his eyes, squinted against the brightness, and yawned. "Where?" he asked.

"Never mind, they're out of sight now," Joe replied.

"Don't worry," Mike said. "You'll see lots of coyotes in this part of the world. Matter of fact, the place we head for on the tour is called Coyote Canyon."

"Coyotes are boring," Jessica said.

"I wouldn't say that too loud, Jessie," Mike replied. "People around here believe that coyotes are mighty smart—*too* smart sometimes."

"That's dumb," Jessica said coldly. "And my name's Jessica, not Jessie."

Frank rubbed his eyes and yawned again, then looked around. They were following a one-lane gravel road that had been cut into the wall of a small canyon. On the driver's side was a rocky slope dotted with straggly bushes. Now and then, their branches brushed against the side of the jeep. The sound reminded Frank of fingernails on a blackboard.

On the right, the ground fell away steeply to a boulder-strewn creek bed fifty feet below. Frank leaned his head out the window and spotted a faint trickle of water at the bottom. In the spring, when the snows melted in the mountains, the creek must be a raging torrent, Frank thought. He'd like to see that someday . . . from a safe vantage.

Frank noticed that the tires of the jeep were speeding along only a few inches from the unguarded edge of the road and the murderous drop beyond. He pulled his head in and reminded himself that Mike drove this road constantly.

"What the—" Mike exclaimed.

From the front seat, Jessica let out a shrill cry.

The jeep was rounding a blind curve. Ahead, only a few dozen feet away, a green pickup truck was completely blocking the road. Mike slammed his foot on the brake pedal. The jeep bucked and began to slide sideways.

"We're going over the cliff!" Jessica screamed. "We'll all be killed!"

2 Howls in the Night

"Hold on, everybody!" Mike shouted. He eased the steering wheel to the left, in the direction of the skid, and started to pump the brakes.

Joe braced his feet against the base of the front seat and gripped the armrest with his left hand. Then he stretched his right arm out in front of Nick, who was sitting in the middle and didn't have a shoulder belt.

Mike managed to bring the jeep to a stop. A choking cloud of red dust drifted through the open windows.

"You guys wait here," Mike growled, throwing his door open and jumping out. Joe noticed that his fists were clenched.

Joe exchanged a lightning glance with Frank, then hit the release of his seat belt and reached for the door handle. As he sprang out, he saw that the jeep was just a few feet from the green pickup and only inches from the edge of the drop.

"That was a close call," he said to Frank, who had circled around the back of the jeep to join him. Nick and Jessica had remained inside.

"It's not over yet," Frank replied.

Mike was striding up the road toward a broad-shouldered man in grease-stained khakis.

"You, Ramirez!" Mike shouted. "What are you doing on my land?"

"It's a public road, last I heard," the man replied. "And I keep good track of where I've a right to go. You know that, Preston."

"Well, get that truck of yours out of the middle of the road. Are you crazy, stopping there? You nearly killed us!"

"Maybe you need some driving lessons," Ramirez said, walking slowly in Mike's direction. "A man can't help it if his truck stalls with vapor lock, can he? Maybe you could do with some politeness lessons, too, and maybe I'm the one to give them to you."

Joe and Frank moved forward, stopping shoulder to shoulder just behind Mike.

Ramirez raised his eyebrows. "Well, well," he drawled. "Hired you some out-of-town muscle, did you? Don't get any ideas, boys," he added. "I can take pretty good care of myself, if I have to."

"We don't want trouble, Ramirez," Mike said. "Just move that heap of yours out of our way."

For a moment, the other man seemed to consider refusing. Then, with a short nod, he said, "I'll do that,

10

Preston, if the truck starts for me. But don't get the idea that it's because you told me to."

As Ramirez climbed into the pickup, Joe glanced at the lettering on the door—Off-Road Adventures—and a picture of a jeep with mountains in the background. Then Joe raised his arm to protect his face, as the pickup took off in a spray of gravel.

"Who's that guy?" Joe asked Mike.

"Roy Ramirez," Mike replied. "His ranch borders mine. He heads up an outfit called Off-Road Adventures that takes teens on expeditions in off-road vehicles."

"A lot like what you do," Frank observed.

Mike looked thoughtful. "Well . . . sort of. We both take teenagers on tours of the mesa country. But the experiences are really different. Being on horseback brings you a lot closer to nature, and our tours have less impact on the environment, too. That's why more kids have been choosing to come with us. We've just been in operation a couple of summers, but we've already pulled in more campers than ORA."

"And Mr. Ramirez isn't too happy about that," Joe suggested.

"No," Mike agreed. "We never got along all that well, and now he's mad enough to chew nails. As a matter of fact, it's crossed my mind that he might have something to do with all these accidents."

"We came very close to another accident just now," Frank pointed out. "A really bad one. And we know that his truck was responsible. Could he have stopped there on purpose?"

11

Mike scratched his chin. "Well . . . hardly anyone uses this road except us. And our one-week tours always start early Monday morning and finish back at the ranch on Friday night. That means most everybody arrives in Durango on either Saturday or Sunday. Roy knows that, of course, and he knows the plane schedules as well as I do."

Joe said, "So he could have been practically certain that you'd be coming along this road at about this time. And he could have left his truck blocking the road, on the far side of a blind curve, hoping you'd either crash or go over the cliff."

Mike frowned. "Roy and I don't see eye to eye," he said. "But I'd hate to believe he'd pull a low-down trick like that. I don't think he'd want to risk hurting innocent kids."

"The trees would have blocked our fall," Joe replied. "And maybe he knew you could stop in time, and just wanted to give you a scare."

"Maybe. But it is a hot day, and it's possible his truck stalled, just like he said," Mike mused as he started for the jeep. "Come on, we'd better head for the ranch. Dotty—that's my wife—will start to wonder where we are."

A few miles farther, Mike turned the jeep to the right at a crossroads, rattled over a row of steel pipes that went across the road, and started down a narrow dirt lane with two strands of barbed wire on each side.

"What was that thing we just crossed?" Nick asked.

"That's a cattle guard," Mike explained. "The

12

pipes are set a few inches apart—just far enough so that cattle won't try to walk over them, but close enough not to bother our horses. We don't keep a herd anymore, but the guards are still there. And there's the ranch, right up ahead."

The ranch house was a long, low wooden building with a steep shingle roof. A trickle of gray smoke came from the big stone chimney at one end. Joe had to remind himself that he hadn't wandered onto the set of a western movie. This really *was* the West.

Mike drove around to the back of the house and parked next to a weathered barn. On the other side of the yard was a long, narrow building with doors that came up only halfway in the openings. Joe decided that it must be the stable. At the sound of the jeep, a black horse with a white blaze on its forehead looked out one of the openings, rolled its eyes, and gave a prolonged snort.

"That's Beauty," Mike said, getting out of the jeep. "She's a real comedian." He opened the trunk to let the teens retrieve their bags. Jessica made a big show of having trouble lifting her suitcase over the trunk rim. Silently Mike helped her.

"Hi there," someone called. "Welcome to Teen Trails West."

Joe turned. A young woman was coming toward them from the house. She had shoulder-length brown hair, brown eyes, and smile lines around her mouth, and she wore jeans, rubber boots, and a Save the Whales T-shirt.

"Hi, sweetie," Mike said. "Sorry we're late. People,

13

meet Dotty." He told her everybody's name. Joe noticed that she gave him and Frank an especially warm smile, with a little hint of conspiracy in it. She must know why we're here, Joe thought.

"Neat shirt," Nick said. "I'm into whales, too. But why are you wearing galoshes? Is it supposed to rain?"

"Barnyards are usually pretty muddy, rain or no rain," Dotty replied.

"Where is everybody?" Mike asked.

"Billy Bob and Tom took the others down to the corral, to meet their mounts," Dotty replied. "They're likely to be there awhile. You might want to join them."

Mike nodded. "Good idea. Everybody, just leave your things here. We can pick them up on our way back to the house."

Jessica peered at the ground and said, "You expect me to put my suitcase down in that yucky mud? Like, look what it did to my shoes. El grosso!"

"You just come along with me, Jessie," Dotty said. "We'll put your valise on the back porch."

As the girl from Beverly Hills trailed after Dotty, lugging her suitcase with both hands, Joe overheard her mutter, "My name's not Jessie, lady. It's Jessica." Apparently this time she didn't have the nerve to say it too loudly.

"You guys come with me," Mike said to Frank, Joe, and Nick. "They can catch up with us."

He led them around the end of the stable and down a short slope. At the bottom was a good-sized meadow, enclosed by a rail fence, holding more than a dozen horses. Some were grazing, and others were standing near the gate, looking at a group of people who were scattered along the fence.

Mike took Nick and the Hardys over to two men at the edge of the group. They looked more like cowhands than city people.

"Joe, Frank, Nick," Mike said, "meet Billy Bob Batten. He's a top amateur rodeo rider, when he's not driving our chuck wagon. He's a fair-to-middling cook, too, but you'll have a chance to judge that for yourselves," he added with a wink. "And this is our chief wrangler, Tom Ouray."

Both men were wearing jeans and boots, but that was the only resemblance Joe could see. Billy Bob was a little under average height, with a snub-nosed, freckled face, ears that stuck out, and a shock of red hair. His boots had colored leather insets of bucking broncos and three elaborate B's in red, white, and blue. Tom, just under six feet, had a massive barrel chest and huge hands. His dark complexion, round face, and hawklike nose would have told Joe that he was of Native American origin, even without the two braids of jet black hair or the silver and turquoise bracelet on his left wrist.

Two teens, a blond, willowy girl and a short, stocky guy with dark hair that nearly met his bushy eyebrows, came over just then.

"Mike?" the girl said with a hint of a southern accent. "Are we going to be near any ruins on our trip?"

15

"Carina loves ruins," her companion confided. He had a twinkle in his eye that suggested he could find the funny side of any situation.

Mike glanced at Tom, who said, "We will pass many sites where people lived a long time ago."

"We will? Really?" Carina exclaimed. "Can we stop and explore? I'll just die, I know I will! I am *so* in love with archaeology!"

Mike interrupted long enough to make a round of introductions. The guy with dark hair was Greg Leboeuf. Carina was his twin sister.

Tom, replying to Carina's earlier question, said, "We'll be exploring some of the ruins, but we'll have to be careful not to disturb anything. Remember, an archaeological site is like an endangered species. Once it is gone, it is gone forever."

"Mike?" A tall, skinny boy of about fifteen came up to them. He had sandy hair, pale blue eyes, and hands that looked too big for his body. "Do we get to choose our own horses for the trip? I really love the big white one."

Mike smiled at the boy, whom he introduced to the newcomers as Alex Adams. "You mean Pom-Pom? Sorry, Alex, but Pom-Pom isn't a saddle horse. He's a draft horse. His job is pulling the chuck wagon."

At the sound of his name, a big white horse trotted over and arched his neck over the fence.

"Meet Pom-Pom," Mike added, scratching the big horse's muzzle.

Joe reached up and patted the side of Pom-Pom's

16

neck. "Wow, is he tall," he said, feeling a little overawed. "I'd hate to have to climb up on his back. It must be like riding an elephant."

Mike smiled. "I reckon you're right. But Pom-Pom wouldn't care to have anybody on his back, anyway. I doubt if he'd stand for it."

Pom-Pom snorted loudly and tossed his head, as if agreeing.

"Hi, I'm Lisa Politano," someone said from behind them. "You guys just get here? Hold it."

Joe turned, just as the speaker snapped a picture. Lisa Politano had dark, wavy hair, dark eyes, and a pro model SLR camera in her hands. She looked as if she knew how to use it.

"Lisa offered to take a lot of pictures for the next Teen Trails West brochure," Mike explained. "This is her second tour this summer. She's becoming a real regular, right?"

"You bet, Mike," Lisa said. She raised her camera and took another picture, just as Jessica joined the group.

"Snapshots?" Jessica drawled. "How quaint."

After a short silence, Mike introduced Jessica to the others. When he got to Carina and Greg, he mentioned that they were twins.

"Oh? I've never understood why people think twins are so interesting," Jessica remarked. "Last year our golden retriever had a litter of eight puppies, but we didn't make a big deal about it."

"I just hope nothing happens to her," Joe muttered

17

to Frank. "If she keeps making enemies at this rate, we'll have so many suspects that we won't have a hope of finding out whodunit."

After a brief tour of the ranch, the group returned to the house for dinner. The meal was served family-style around a long table.

Following dinner, everyone gathered in the main room around the fireplace. The big room was lit only by the flickering flames. Joe sat on the floor between Nick and Carina. Frank was on the other side of the little semicircle, near the window.

"Tom?" Mike said, after everyone settled down. "Do you feel like favoring us with a story? Tom's father is an elder, a wise man of the Ute culture," he added, looking around the semicircle of faces. "Until the Europeans came, all this part of the country was Ute territory."

"Yes," Tom said in a deep voice. "This is true. But before *we* came here, many hundreds of years before, this was home to a people we know as the Anasazi. Before they went away, they built the great cliff dwellings of Mesa Verde and Chaco Canyon, and many smaller towns and villages as well. As I told Carina before, we will pass many of them on our expedition this week."

"I can't wait," Carina said.

Tom smiled at her and continued. "Tonight I want to tell you a story I learned from my grandfather, who learned it from *his* grandfather. Who knows? Maybe it was even told in the villages of the Anasazi, a thousand years ago. It is the story of why Coyote, the Trickster, howls at the sky. Coyote is called the Trickster because he is very smart and very sly. But sometimes he ends up outsmarting himself, as you will hear."

As Joe listened to Tom, he also studied the others in the group. Carina, Alex, and Nick seemed enthralled by the ancient tale of a time before there were stars in the sky. Jessica was frowning down at her nails, as if wondering how far it was to the nearest manicurist. Greg was looking across at Jessica, as if wondering what planet she had dropped down from. Billy Bob was sitting a little away from the others, looking deep in thought.

Tom explained how a wise bear had found shining stones in a river and thrown them into the sky, where they made a picture of the bear in points of light. "When the bear told the other animals what he had done," Tom continued, "they wanted to do the same, but they were too small to do as the bear had done. So they gathered many of the shining stones and took them to Coyote, the Trickster, and asked him to draw their portraits in the sky.

Tom paused and looked at the group, then went on. "Coyote took the bag of stones and went to work, but after the first few, he became tired. It will take me many nights of much effort to throw all these stones, one by one, Coyote thought. So he opened the bag and threw all the stones at once. The star-stones swirled around in the sky until they settled into patterns . . . but not pictures.

19

"The other animals were very angry that they were not drawn in the heavens, the way the Great Bear was. They were angry, too, that they had trusted Coyote. He laughed at their anger, but then he realized that he had not drawn his own portrait with the star-stones, either. And ever since then, on starry nights—"

Tom broke off in the middle of the sentence and raised his head to look toward the window. The others in the little semicircle turned that way, too. Joe looked, but he couldn't see anything out of the ordinary—only a window seat and a wide window with café curtains, and the darkness outside.

Then he heard it. Somewhere in the distance, a coyote was howling. Another joined it, then another.

The hair on the back of Joe's neck stood up. "There must be dozens of coyotes out there," he said, exchanging a glance with his brother.

"And they seem to be coming closer," Frank added.

The sound was getting louder and louder, as if the wild animals were all coming straight toward the house!

3 Four-Legged Terror

"What's that noise?" Jessica cried. "It's coming closer!"

Nick was staring wide eyed at the window, looking excited and nervous. "I've never heard coyotes in New York City," he said with a gulp. The other teens were glancing anxiously at Mike.

Mike sprang to his feet. "I'm getting my rifle," he said. "A couple of shots in the air ought to scare those coyotes off. I won't have them spooking my horses."

"Coyotes never come so close to people's houses," Tom said. "That's something else out there."

"What do you think it is?" Alex asked, with a hint of tremor in his voice. His pale blue eyes darted to the window.

"I don't know," Tom replied, getting to his feet. "It sounds a lot like coyotes, but—"

"I think I know what it is," Frank said. He jumped up from his place on the floor and walked quickly to the window. When he got there, the sounds faded to silence. He scanned the windowframe and felt under the curtains, then took a step backward. The panels along the front of the window seat had many small holes drilled in them, in curving patterns.

"What's under there?" Frank asked Mike.

"Nothing, now," Mike replied. "There used to be a radiator, but we tore it out years ago, when we replaced the old coal furnace. Why?"

In answer, Frank tugged at the front edge of the window seat. The top swung upward on concealed hinges. He bent down and felt around, then straightened up. He held a battery-powered cassette player in his hand.

"Is this yours, Tom?" he asked, holding it up. "I don't think you needed the extra atmosphere. You were telling a terrific story without it."

"I've never seen that before," Tom said coldly. "And I do not play tricks on people."

Frank pressed Rewind, then Play. Suddenly the room was filled with the yelps and howls of a pack of coyotes. Frank pressed Stop. "*Someone* is playing tricks," he pointed out. "And I don't think the coyote in your story owns a cassette player."

"That's mine," Billy Bob said, from his place at the far side of the room. "I put it there just before you all came in to hear Tom's story."

22

"You, Billy Bob?" Mike demanded. "Why did you do a thing like that?"

"I thought it would liven things up," the chuck wagon cook admitted with a shrug. "I figured once we were all around the fire, Tom would tell his coyote story, the way he always does. Then it came to me that hearing some coyote sounds would make it more real. I guess it was a pretty poor idea. I'm sorry if I scared anybody."

When the gathering broke up for the night, Joe held Frank back. "How did you guess about that stupid stunt of Billy Bob's?" he asked Frank. "It sure had me fooled."

"Me, too," Frank admitted. "But then I noticed that all the sounds were coming from exactly the same direction. That meant the sound had to be from a single source, such as a loudspeaker. The only other possibility was that the coyotes had joined a college marching band and learned to parade in single file."

Joe laughed. "We were lucky," he said. "Just think if Billy Bob's machine had been stereo."

Frank's expression turned somber, as he followed his brother to the bunkhouse. "But seriously, Joe. I wonder just how innocent Billy Bob's little trick was."

Somewhere nearby, a bell clanged repeatedly. Frank rolled over, sat up, and rubbed his eyes. Outside the bunkhouse window, mountains showed dark against a pink eastern sky. Frank yawned and stretched. How early is it, anyway? he wondered.

The door of the room banged open. "Shake a leg,

23

buckaroos!" Mike called from the doorway. "Rise and shine."

Joe groaned from the lower bunk. "I don't believe it. Nobody calls people 'buckaroos,' especially at three in the morning."

"It's five-thirty, and time for breakfast," Mike replied. "Come and get it, before we throw it out."

"Is that a promise?" Nick asked feebly from the top bunk on the other side of the room.

In response, Mike crossed the bunk room and pulled the blankets off Nick. Then, for good measure, he pulled the blankets off Alex, in the bunk under Nick's. He was reaching for Greg's when the teen sat up, hands in the air, and cried out, "I surrender!"

Mike laughed and left the room, saying over his shoulder, "Three minutes, then I come after you with a bucket of cold water."

Frank and the other guys got out of bed and struggled into their clothes. As soon as they were dressed, they found their way to the dining room.

Dotty was just putting a platter of scrambled eggs and sausage on the buffet at the side of the room, next to a plate stacked high with toast.

"Help yourselves," she said. "These jams and jellies are made right here on the ranch. And there's home-made yogurt and granola from our secret recipe, too."

Frank filled a plate and carried it to the table. The nearest free place was between Alex and Carina.

"Hi," he said as he sat down. "Are you two looking forward to this trip as much as I am?"

24

Alex made a face and said, "That depends if we're expected to get up this early every day."

"We'll be getting to sleep earlier, too," Carina pointed out. "After six or eight hours in the saddle, we'll be tuckered out."

"Where are you from, Carina?" Frank asked. He thought he knew already from her accent.

"Greg and I, we're from Louisiana, down in 'gator country," she replied. "Just a couple of swamp rats. So you can imagine what those big mountains out there look like to us. We never saw the like in our lives."

"I'm from St. Louis," Alex volunteered. "Just up the Mississippi from you guys. It's pretty flat around there, too."

"And my brother and I are from Bayport, New York," Frank offered. "Also flat. That's five out of eight so far, and Nick is from New York City, so that's six out of eight. I guess people who already live in the mountains wouldn't get so excited by the idea of a week-long horseback ride through the high country."

From across the table, Lisa said, "Make that seven out of eight. Cleveland isn't totally flat, but it's nothing like this, that's for sure."

"Who does that leave?" Alex asked, as he looked around the room. "Oh," he added, apparently noticing Jessica, who was standing at the buffet complaining to Dotty about the breakfast selections.

"She's from Beverly Hills, and her family has a place in the Sierras," Carina said in a low voice, leaning forward. "We heard all about it last night, while we were trying to get some sleep. So there goes Frank's theory about the people who sign up for this being flatlanders."

Lisa whispered, "Not necessarily. From something she said last night, I don't think Jessica signed up on her own. I think somebody else, like her parents, signed her up."

Carina raised her eyebrows. "For her own good, you mean?"

"Isn't that what they always say?" Alex said in an undertone. "I just wish—"

Mike tapped his fork against his juice glass. The table fell silent.

"We're all going to have a great time this week," Mike began. "Right now I want to give you a general idea of what's in store. We'll be making a big loop to the west of here, through mesa country. It's isolated and it's rugged, but I think it's about as beautiful as anything you'll find anywhere in the U.S. of A."

"Anywhere in the world," Dotty added.

Mike smiled. "We'll be packing in everything we need on the trip, and packing out all our garbage. At Teen Trails West, we're proud to say that someone crossing our tracks a week or a month from now won't even know we've been by there."

"Or care," Jessica muttered from the buffet, just loud enough for Mike, and everyone else, to hear.

"First thing this morning," Mike continued, ignoring her, "we'll have a quick lesson in saddling and bridling your mounts. You'll all get to be real close to your horses over the next few days, and you'll want to know how to care for them properly. After that, we hit the trail. Any questions?" Mike asked, taking a sip of his coffee.

"What about Indian ruins?" Carina asked. "Will we see any today?"

"We might," Mike replied. "But let me say something about that. For most of this trip, we'll be on public lands, overseen by the Bureau of Land Management. And there are very strict federal laws against disturbing archaeological sites on public lands. You're free to look around, but don't move or disturb *anything*, not even a stone."

After breakfast, Mike and Tom took everyone out to the corral and began matching riders and horses, according to each rider's level of skill and experience. Frank and Joe were given lively, spirited mounts. Frank's was a big black named Star, because of the white star on his forehead. Joe's horse, Magic, was white with a silky white mane and tail.

After everyone got acquainted with their horses, with the help of some carrots and sugar cubes, the group saddled up and hit the trail. Dotty, who was staying at the ranch to handle the business end of Teen Trails West, stood on the veranda and waved them off.

Frank was riding near the back of the line. When not looking at the scenery, he studied the others in the group. Nick and Jessica were both good riders, though Nick looked happier in the saddle than Jessica, who seemed tense. Lisa and Alex looked comfortable, too. Greg and Carina, the Leboeuf twins, were both inexperienced. Mike had given them horses that were so gentle and well trained that their riders hardly needed to know which end of the horse was which.

An hour after the group left the ranch, Mike called a fifteen-minute halt. "Stretch your legs," he advised, as people clambered down off their horses. "Don't stay too still, or you'll start to stiffen up."

Tom strung a rope between two piñon trees and tied the horses to it.

"I already stiffened up." Joe groaned, flexing his knees. "Are we really going to do this all day?"

"Yup," Mike replied cheerfully. "And every day this week. Don't worry, it'll seem easier once you get used to it."

Frank stepped aside to let Lisa snap a close-up of Mike. Then she backed away to get a shot of the whole group.

"Smile!" she commanded. After clicking the shutter, she said, "Nick, what are you doing? You ruined my picture! You had your sweater up over your face."

Nick looked at her, then at the sweater in his hand, and said, "Sorry, Lisa. I was too hot with it on. I'll go put it away in my pack."

He walked over to the chuck wagon, which contained all the baggage. A couple of minutes later, he returned with a worried expression on his face.

"My pack isn't in the wagon," Nick announced. "I don't see my sleeping bag, either."

Frank caught Joe's eye, then stepped forward. "Are you sure, Nick?"

"Of course I am," Nick replied. "I helped load the wagon. My pack was right near the top of the pile. And the whole pile looks smaller than it was. I think there's a bunch of stuff missing."

Mike hurried over to the wagon. Frank and Joe were right behind him, followed by the others. After a quick count, Mike said, "Nick's right. There should be a dozen packs here, and I only see nine. The rest must have been left behind somehow."

"What about my clothes?" Jessica demanded. "You can't expect me to go for days without a change of outfit!"

"Yours is here," Mike said wryly. "I noticed it. It's the only suitcase in the bunch."

"I *know* we loaded everything," Nick insisted.

"Never mind," Tom said quickly. "I'll ride back to the ranch and take a look around." He headed toward his horse, a tall sorrel.

An hour later, as the group was turning onto a trail that led down into a narrow valley between two mesas, Tom caught up to them. Frank saw that he had the missing packs strapped to his horse's back.

"It's okay," Tom said loudly. "I've got everything."

Billy Bob stopped the chuck wagon in a small clearing, and Tom put the missing packs aboard. Then, while Nick and the other teens gathered around the chuck wagon to check on their belongings, Tom, Mike, Frank, and Joe led their horses to a secluded spot.

"Where did you find the packs?" Mike asked Tom. "How did they come to be left behind?"

"Beats me," Tom replied in a low voice. "They were in the bushes, right next to where the wagon was parked this morning."

"*In* the bushes, or *under* the bushes?" Frank demanded.

Tom gave him a sharp glance, then looked questioningly at Mike.

"Frank and Joe are friends," Mike said. "You can talk to them."

"Well, all right then. Under the bushes," Tom admitted with a slow nod. "They didn't just fall off the wagon, if that's what you're asking. The way it looks to me, somebody must have deliberately slung them there."

"Nick and Lisa helped Billy Bob load the wagon," Joe pointed out. "Any one of them could have done it."

"Without the others seeing?" Mike asked skeptically.

Frank came to his brother's defense. "It's just possible," he said. "Let's say I sling a pack into the wagon, but I keep a grip on the strap. Then, the second your back is turned, I pull it out again and toss it under the bushes. You might not notice."

"Once, maybe not," Mike insisted. "But three times? Come on, give me a break."

30

"Anyway, it didn't have to happen like that," Tom said. "The way the chuck wagon was sitting, between the bushes and the yard, anybody who walked around to that side could have done whatever he wanted, without much reason to worry about somebody seeing him."

Frank frowned thoughtfully. "Then you think that after Lisa, Nick, and Billy Bob loaded the packs, but before we all mounted up, somebody else sneaked around to that side of the wagon, pulled out some of the packs, and hid them under the bushes?" Somebody like Ramirez, he added silently.

"That's right," Tom replied. "Except there's nothing to say it wasn't Lisa or Nick or Billy Bob who did the sneaking and hiding."

"There's nothing to say who it *was*, either," Mike said, in a voice full of frustration.

"We can try to narrow it down," Joe offered. "We're just talking about fifteen minutes or so. There must be some people who were together that whole time. We could eliminate them."

"Unless they're in cahoots," Tom objected.

Mike threw up his hands. "All these maybes and unlesses. I'd rather deal with a flash flood or a stampede any day of the week and twice on Sunday."

He picked up the reins and tapped his heels against his horse's sides. "Let's move out," he said. "It's not that long till noon, and we're still an hour or more from the overlook, where we're supposed to stop for lunch."

31

As they rode, Frank noticed the surroundings. The trail they were following led down into a valley between two mesas. The walls of the valley were mostly bare rock, in shades of yellow, orange, and red. Here and there, an especially hardy bush sprouted from among the boulders.

Up ahead, the valley broadened out, giving him a view of more mesas. Frank remembered that the previous night someone had mentioned that *mesa* was the Spanish word for table. He could see how they got the name. The sides of the tall mountains were jagged and steep, but the tops, green with low trees, were perfectly flat. All of the mesas were about the same height, too. He imagined a giant dragging a sharp stick through a level plain, leaving deep gouges behind. The ungouged spots would be the mesas. It occurred to him that his image wasn't so inaccurate. Once powerful rivers had eroded the deep valleys between the mesas.

The group reached the overlook after noon. It was a level, triangular point of land that jutted out into a narrow valley with red rock walls. On one side of the overlook, a gravel-covered hillside sloped steeply down to the valley floor. The other side was a rocky cliff.

"If this was Europe, I bet there'd be an old castle on top of this rock," Carina said as she helped Frank spread the plastic tablecloths for their picnic lunch. "Wouldn't that be romantic?"

"Huh! You'd have to be nuts to want to live around here, even in a castle," Jessica said. "I bet you'd have to drive a hundred miles just to get your hair trimmed and styled."

"You learn to cope," Mike said, giving Frank a grin. "Dotty does her own hair, and gives me my haircuts, too."

Jessica silently studied Mike's head, then gave a single, scornful sniff.

"I reckon I don't live up to her standards," Mike joked to Frank. "There goes that part I was hoping for in one of her daddy's movies."

Lunch was sandwiches and fruit. After a short pause for picture taking and a careful cleanup of the area, Mike called, "Okay, let's mount up!"

Frank and Joe retrieved their horses, Star and Magic. They were the first of the group to finish saddling up. Frank swung up onto his horse, then noticed that Joe was having a problem mounting. Magic kept circling and backing away. Finally Joe managed to grab the bridle right next to the bit and hold the horse still long enough to get his left foot into the stirrup.

"Easy, boy," he murmured as he hoisted himself into the saddle.

Suddenly Magic gave a loud snort and bolted. Joe grabbed the saddle horn and kept his seat, but lost his hold on the reins.

"Whoa, boy, whoa!" Joe cried out. He saw with horror that the horse was running straight toward the edge of the little plateau, which was a steep drop down. Both he and the horse would be in great danger if they went over the edge!

4 Another Deadly Ride

Frank urged Star forward, hoping to get between Joe and the edge of the slope, but Lisa and her mount had drifted right in front of him. He had to rein in to keep from colliding with them. Star, upset by the shouting and sudden movements, rolled his eyes and began to lurch backward. Frank tried to get him moving forward again, but Star would not cooperate.

Joe's horse, Magic, was only twenty feet from the edge now. Suddenly Billy Bob ran out from behind the chuck wagon with a tablecloth in his hands. He flapped it in front of the spooked horse, who reared on its hind legs. Joe managed to hold on, and the horse came down on all fours and began bucking and neighing frantically.

Tom dashed up and grabbed Magic's bridle with both hands. "Jump!" he shouted to Joe. "I'll try to hold him still!"

Instantly Joe swung his leg over the saddle horn and dived for the ground, finishing with a quick tuck and roll.

Mike was at Tom's side, helping him hold and soothe the frightened horse. Magic tried to back away from them, then stood still.

Frank quickly dismounted and hitched Star to the wheel of the chuck wagon, then hurried over to Joe. "Are you okay?" he demanded.

Joe got to his feet and brushed himself off. "I guess so," he replied, eyeing Magic. "But I just found out something important. Somebody forgot to install the emergency brake on that thing."

Frank and Joe joined Mike and Tom, who were tending Joe's horse. The others were off to the side, talking nervously among themselves.

"I don't get it," Tom was saying. "Magic's never given us a minute of trouble up till now."

"Too bad Magic can't tell us what's wrong," Mike said. "Joe, you didn't notice any problem before, did you?"

"Nope. Magic was doing fine until just now." Joe reached up to stroke his horse's neck, resting his other hand on the saddle horn. Magic snorted loudly and tried to edge away.

"There's something wrong with the saddle," Frank said. "Is the girth strap too tight?"

Tom put his fingers under the edge of the strap. "Feels fine to me," he said. "But let's get this saddle off. Maybe he's got a burr in his blanket."

He loosened the strap, lifted off the saddle, and passed it to Joe. As he pulled off the saddle blanket, Magic danced away. At the same moment, Tom cried out, dropped the blanket to the ground, and looked at his fingertip. Frank looked, too, and saw a drop of blood.

Mike picked up the blanket and felt along the edges. Then he pulled out a shiny straight pin.

"What's that doing there?" Joe demanded.

"That's what I want to know," Mike said grimly. "There's more of them, too." He pulled three out and held them up for Tom and the Hardys to see.

"Could the pins have been there all morning, without Magic noticing?" Frank asked. "Otherwise, they must have been put there while we were having lunch."

"Well . . ." Mike replied. "The edge binding is pretty thick material, and horses have pretty thick hides. I guess if the pin was lying sideways, instead of sticking straight down, it might not bother the horse any. You're thinking that somebody put them there on purpose, to spook Joe's horse?"

"It's pretty obvious, isn't it?" Frank replied.

"The material around the edge of the saddle blanket looks new," Joe remarked.

"It is," Tom said. "I put new borders on some of the worn blankets yesterday morning, and this is one of

36

them. But I didn't leave any pins in them," he stated firmly.

Mike looked at him with a troubled expression, then said, "I know you didn't, Tom. All the same, I think we'd better check the other blankets you worked on. We don't want any more accidents."

Frank and Joe followed them as they went from horse to horse. Tom pointed out three more blankets that he had repaired. All of them had two or three pins stuck in the hems. The others in the group stood in a little cluster, watching silently.

"This is crazy," Tom protested. "I wouldn't have forgotten even one pin, never mind nearly a dozen of them!"

"Those pins didn't get there by themselves," Mike said grimly.

"Did anyone know you were working on these particular saddle blankets?" Joe asked.

Tom scowled. "I was sitting outside the stable while I worked. Just about everybody walked by me at one time or another."

"Where did you put the saddle blankets when you finished with them?" Frank asked.

"Back in the tack room, with all the others."

"In a stack?" Frank continued.

"Nope. I slung one over each of the saddles. That's the way I usually do it."

Joe asked, "Is there a way of telling which saddle goes with which horse?"

"Why, sure," Mike replied. "They're labeled. But

if you're thinking somebody was out to get you in particular, you're wrong. Nobody knew till this morning who'd end up with which mount."

"But he or she *could* have known that Magic would be assigned to one of the more skilled riders, correct?" Frank said. "So he or she may have figured that the pins would cause a scary, but not a serious, incident. The person couldn't have known that Magic would bolt near a steep drop."

"It was still a pretty nasty thing to do," Joe said. "If you guys hadn't stopped Magic when you did, he would have carried me over the edge. We'd both be in pretty bad shape right now."

"I hear what you're saying," Mike said. "I guess we'd better check all the saddle blankets for pins, and not just the ones Tom rehemmed."

But none of the other blankets had pins in their hems. Frank gave Tom a thoughtful look. No question that he had had the best opportunity to stick the pins in the blankets. Not only was he in charge of all the riding gear, he had actually been sewing those very blankets. But would he have dared to pull a trick that pointed so clearly to him? It didn't seem likely . . . unless he was counting on others to reason exactly that way!

Mike returned to his horse and mounted up. "Okay, gang," he called, "we're on our way."

Tom led the group. Mike, Frank, and Joe waited until the last of the riders had passed, then fell in a dozen feet behind. The trail was wide enough for the three of them to ride side by side.

"You're beginning to see what I mean," Mike said gloomily. "It was just through pure luck that Joe didn't have a really serious accident."

Frank pounded his fist against his thigh in frustration. "Let's say Tom didn't do it. That means the pins had to be put there sometime after noon yesterday. Otherwise Tom would have found them and taken them out. So anyone who was at the ranch either yesterday or today could have slipped into the tack room and stuck the pins in the blankets. It wouldn't have taken more than a couple of minutes."

Joe said, "My guess is that our trickster got the idea from seeing Tom sewing the blankets. That means that Nick and Jessica are in the clear, since they weren't there yesterday morning. And what about Ramirez? Could he have sneaked onto the ranch without anyone noticing?"

"I'm glad you're the detectives and not me," Mike remarked. "With all these twists and turns, I'd go loco inside of an hour. Excuse me, I'd better check on how the others are making out." He made a clicking sound with his tongue, and his horse broke into a trot.

"I think I'll go get better acquainted with some of the gang," Joe told Frank, looking up ahead at the line of riders. "Carina's the closest."

"Good idea," Frank replied. "I'll do the same."

Joe rode ahead. Frank waited a few moments, then edged past Joe and Carina to a place in line just behind Alex and Jessica. He was close enough to overhear their conversation.

"I can't believe I'm actually here," Alex was saying.

"A girl I know was on the tour last year. After she told me how great it was, I spent the last ten months trying to talk my parents into sending me. Can you believe the scenery? Look at that view!"

"It's okay if you're, like, into rocks," Jessica drawled. "I think they're boring."

Alex seemed determined to be friendly to her. "And I'm finally on a real trail ride," he continued. "It's just like the old West. Hey, I noticed you ride really well. Do you do a lot of riding?"

"Everybody I know rides," Jessica replied. "I used to have my own horse, but I got tired of it. I made Daddy sell it and buy me a convertible instead."

"Oh, yeah? I don't know if I'd have done that," Alex said. "It's true you don't have to feed and brush a convertible every day. But it's never glad to see you, either. It doesn't honk its horn when you walk into the garage and come over to see if you've got an apple for it."

"My horse wasn't a pet," Jessica replied coolly. "She was a very highly trained show horse, a champion at dressage. We were more like teammates than friends, so it was no big deal to get rid of her."

"Uh-huh," Alex said. "Hey, I just remembered something I wanted to tell Greg."

Before Jessica could reply, he urged his horse forward. She was left with no one to ride with.

Frank found himself wondering about her. Why did she seem so determined to turn off everyone who came near her? Was she really as bored and unhappy —and spoiled—as she seemed? Or was she putting on an act for some reason?

Frank waited a couple of minutes, then moved up alongside her. "Hi, Jessica," he said. "Having fun?"

"What do *you* think?" she asked, curling her lip. "Stuck out in the wilderness, hundreds of miles from a decent mall, with a bunch of dweebs?"

Frank chose a direct approach. "If that's the way you feel, I'm surprised you decided to come."

"Decided? Very funny! Mums thought it would be good for me. You know, like fresh air and exercise and sleeping under the stars? And wholesome kids from all over? I told her I was allergic to wholesome, but she said that was my problem. When I said I would totally die, she told me that was too bad, I was going, anyway. Either that, or she'd take away my car, my phone, and my charge cards. So here I am. I mean, what would *you* do?"

"Good question," Frank said, hedging. He crossed off his earlier idea about Jessica. If she was putting this on, she was such a talented actress that she'd surely be a star by now—especially with the help she'd get from Daddy, the Hollywood director!

"I don't know if I can stand it, though," she continued. "Like, everybody here is such a *baby*. Okay, Billy Bob is kind of cute, but how can you take a guy seriously with a dumbo name like that?"

41

Frank laughed out loud. Greg, just ahead in the line, looked back curiously.

"That big blond guy is your brother, isn't he?" she asked suddenly. "How old is he?"

"Seventeen," Frank replied.

"Really? Hmm . . . Does he work out a lot?"

"You can ask him yourself," Frank said.

"I think I will." She touched the rein to her horse's neck and edged off the trail, letting Frank ride on. He looked back, just as she moved in next to Joe. Frank shook his head and laughed to himself.

In the middle of the afternoon, the group took a break near a deep natural pool shaded by cottonwood trees. Everyone watered their horses, then Tom tied them up in the shade. Nick, Greg, and Carina changed into suits and dived in. The others sat on the bank, watching and swapping jokes.

Soon it was time to mount up for the last leg of the day's ride. Frank got into the saddle, noticing a few sore places, and stayed near the horses, chatting with Tom.

Jessica came over to take her horse. Holding the reins and the saddle horn in her left hand, she put her foot in the stirrup and swung herself upward. Suddenly the saddle slipped sideways. Caught off balance, Jessica fell backward, but instead of landing, she hung there upside down. Only her head and shoulders touched the ground.

Frank gasped. Jessica's ankle was trapped in the stirrup!

Startled, her horse jerked its head up, snorted, and lunged forward. Jessica screamed as her shoulders scraped across the stony ground. Her face was only inches from the steel-shod hooves. In another instant, she would be dragged or trampled to death!

5 The Figure on the Hill

Frank swung the reins to the left and dug his heels into Star's flanks. Star sprang forward and to the left, cutting in front of Jessica's horse, who stopped short and reared back.

Tom lunged forward and grabbed the frightened mare's bridle. Joe and Billy Bob came running over. Joe caught Jessica under the arms and held her up off the ground, while Billy Bob worked to get her foot out of the stirrup.

At last she was free. Joe helped her to stand up. She sobbed and clung to his shoulder.

"Are you okay?" Mike demanded.

"I don't know," she said, her voice shaking. She let go of Joe's shoulder and took a wobbly step. Mike caught her as she started to slump to the ground.

"I think you'd better take a couple of minutes to recover," Mike told her. "That was a very scary experience. Dangerous, too. I'm glad Frank was there to help."

Wiping her tears away, Jessica glanced over at Frank, swallowed, and said, "Yeah, thanks." She sounded as if the words had been dragged out of her.

"Glad to be of help," Frank replied. He dismounted and went over to Jessica's horse. The saddle had twisted all the way under the horse's belly. When Frank grasped the cinch strap, he was able to get his whole hand under it without any effort. No wonder the saddle had slipped when Jessica tried to mount up.

Tom saw, too. "Listen, Jessica," he said. "From now on, before you mount up, check to see that your cinch strap is good and tight, will you? You could have really hurt yourself, and your mount, too."

Jessica's face changed from white to red. "It *was* tight," she insisted in a shrill voice. "It was fine before we stopped to rest. Somebody fiddled with it, and I know who!"

She looked around the growing circle of spectators, then shot out her hand and pointed at Alex.

"You've got it in for me," she said loudly. "You kept making nasty remarks when we were talking on the trail. And you were hanging around my horse before. I saw you. You loosened that strap, didn't you?"

Alex stared at her for a moment, then gave a short laugh. "You're out of your gourd, Jessica," he said. "Don't go blaming me because you made a mistake.

Horses take more care than convertibles, you know. Just pay more attention next time."

"Well?" Jessica said, turning to Mike. "You heard him. Aren't you going to do anything? Why don't you arrest him?"

Mike took a deep breath. "First of all," he said, "I'm not a policeman. Second, even if I were, I hope I wouldn't go around arresting a person just because someone accused him of something. There's such a thing as evidence, and so far I haven't seen any."

"You're against me, too!" Jessica exclaimed. "You just wait until I tell my daddy. Wait until I tell the papers about the kind of operation you're running. You'll be sorry." She spun on her heel and rushed away.

Mike took off his ten-gallon hat, scratched his head, and looked around the circle until his gaze met Frank's. "You figure you can do something with that one?" he asked. "You just helped keep her from getting her head busted open, after all. That ought to count for something."

"I'll give it a try," Frank promised. Privately he thought that his chances of calming Jessica down were about as good as his chances of doing a one-arm handstand on the saddle horn while Star was galloping at full speed.

He found Jessica sitting by the edge of the water with her knees clasped in her arms. He sat down in the grass next to her. "I'm glad you weren't hurt," he said.

She looked over at him with her lower lip sticking

out, then looked away again. "No, you aren't," she said. "You don't care about me. Nobody here does." She picked up a small rock and threw it angrily into the water.

"Why do you think Alex has it in for you?" Frank asked.

"The way he talked to me. He thinks I'm mean because I sold a horse I didn't like. What business is it of his? He's just envious. Hey, is it my fault if I live in Beverly Hills and I've been in movies and all?"

"You can envy somebody without doing something dangerous like loosening her saddle strap," Frank pointed out. "You don't really have any proof that Alex did it, do you?"

"I *knew* you were on their side!" Jessica exclaimed. "Just wait till I get to a telephone. I'm going to let all the papers know what's been going on. My daddy will sue every one of you."

Frank took a deep breath and let it out slowly. "I don't think that would be a very good idea," he said. "Bad publicity could do a lot of harm. You wouldn't want to destroy Mike's business, just because you didn't want to come on this trip."

"Oh? Just wait!"

The conversation was every bit as pointless as Frank had expected. "It's time to leave," he said, getting to his feet. "Are you coming?"

"What do you think?" she replied, scrambling up. "I want to get this stupid trip over with!"

* * *

For the rest of the afternoon, the riders followed a leisurely course alongside the stream that ran the length of the valley. A moment of excitement came when a jackrabbit jumped up, practically under the hooves of Joe's horse. While Joe got his horse back under control, the others cheered the rabbit's great display of broken field running.

A little later, Frank was riding next to Carina. Suddenly she let out a gasp and cried, "I don't believe it!"

"What is it?" Frank demanded. Dreading another accident, he looked around quickly. "What's wrong?"

"Look!" she exclaimed, pointing to the cliff that bordered the valley. "Up there."

Frank turned in his saddle. After a moment, he saw a pattern of intersecting straight lines and dark, rectangular holes on part of the cliff face. He realized that he must be looking at a stone wall, complete with small windows. There were shadowed gaps at the top, where the wall no longer joined the cliff face.

"There must be a cave behind that wall," Carina said excitedly. "Maybe more than one. That's one of the ways the cliff dwellers made things easier for themselves, by using caves that were already there and just shutting them off across the front. Oh, I wish we could stop and explore."

"I'm sure we'll have a chance at some point," Frank said. "If we didn't, it would be like signing up for a week at the beach and then being told you couldn't go swimming."

Carina gave him a warm smile. "You do understand, don't you?" she said. "It was all my idea to come on a Teen Trails tour, you know. I could tell from the map in the brochure that we'd be going right through Anasazi country. Greg didn't mind—he likes riding, and roughing it, and all—but what he really likes is playing music, hanging around with other musicians. I was the one who pushed it. I'm planning to be an archaeologist."

"That sounds really exciting," Frank said.

"Oh, it is," she replied. "I could talk about archaeology for hours. But don't worry," she added hastily with a grin, "I won't!"

The sun was already close to the horizon when the group stopped for the night, at a place where the valley widened. Everyone helped set up camp. The tents were pitched in a row, along the bank of the stream. Billy Bob parked the chuck wagon on the other side of the clearing and got to work on cooking a dinner of hash with biscuits, while Tom tethered the horses a little downstream. With help from Greg and Nick, Mike built a campfire in the center of the clearing and got it going, just as Billy Bob called them all to supper.

Everyone filled his or her plate and sat on the ground near the fire to eat—everyone except Lisa, who kept taking pictures of them, the campfire, the chuck wagon, and the surrounding scenery until Mike ordered her to stop and eat dinner.

After his first helping of hash, Joe called out, "How about a big hand for the cook?"

49

Everyone laughed and applauded as Billy Bob took a bow.

"Mike?" Carina said a few minutes later. "I noticed some ruins, up on one of the cliffs, a couple of miles back. Are they very old?"

"I'll let Tom answer that," Mike said. "He's our expert on Native Americans. And not just because his ancestors lived around here. He's done a lot of studying about the history of the region. What about it, Tom?"

Tom was hunkered down, sitting easily on his heels, with his plate balanced on his knees. Just looking at his position made Frank's calves start to ache.

"You have good eyes, Carina," Tom said, turning to the budding archaeologist. "That site we passed a little while back *is* old—and almost certainly Anasazi. That is the name the Navajo gave to the people who built the cities at Mesa Verde and Chaco Canyon," he added, looking around his circle of listeners. Everyone edged in a little closer, except Jessica, who was sitting a little apart, filing her nails. "No one knows what name they called themselves."

"Why not ask them?" Alex suggested.

"Because they vanished," Tom replied solemnly. "Hundreds of years ago, they abandoned their great cities, their hundreds of villages, their network of roads, their terraced gardens, their holy places, and went . . . no one knows where. Some say that a long dry spell forced them to move south, where they became what we now call the Pueblo people. Others say they were destroyed by famine or disease or enemies. Once I met a man who swore that they had been taken away by creatures from another world."

Several people chuckled.

"That explanation *is* a little unlikely," Tom admitted with a grin. "But where so little is known for sure, even the most fantastic explanations can seem possible."

"If these people vanished, and they didn't leave any records, how do we know so much about them?" Nick asked.

Tom smiled. "Carina? Can you answer that?"

Carina's face lit up. "Sure! That's what archaeology is all about—looking at the evidence that people leave behind and figuring out what it tells us about them."

"Evidence?" Lisa asked, puzzled. "You mean like fingerprints?"

"Anything can be evidence," Tom replied. "Suppose you find a bit of a broken pot near here, and you know from the design on it that it came from Chaco Canyon, in New Mexico. Then you know that the people here had some contact and trade with the people of Chaco Canyon. If you find a layer of ashes and scorched stones at the same level in different parts of a village, you can guess that the village suffered a terrible fire, and if you find scorched spear points or arrowheads at the same level, you can guess that the fire was set by attacking enemies. You see?"

Frank nodded. What Tom was describing was really just good detective work.

"That's why it's so important to protect archaeological sites," Tom continued. "What counts isn't just the things that are found, it's the exact spot *where* they're found. Once somebody messes with the evidence, an important clue to our history is lost forever."

"Who would want to mess with the evidence?" Lisa asked. "And why?"

Tom shook his head sadly. "Some, because they don't know any better. The ones I detest do it for the money. As in many cultures, the Anasazi often buried prize possessions in the graves of their important people: fine pieces of pottery, carved turquoise jewelry, baskets, turkey-feather robes . . . These relics are very valuable. A single Anasazi pot might sell for thirty thousand—or even as much as a hundred thousand, if it's really fine."

Lisa gasped, and Alex let out a low whistle.

Jessica looked up from her nails and said, "Hey, okay! And they're just lying around, waiting for somebody to pick them up? Let's go!"

"That's a *terrible* attitude," Carina told her. "Didn't you hear anything Tom said?"

"Sure, Miss Goody-Goody," Jessica retorted. "I heard him. He said just one moldy old pot is worth more than enough to buy a new Porsche. So why not go looking for them? They're not doing anyone any good buried in the ground, are they?"

"I can think of at least three reasons, Jessica," Tom said. "First of all, it's illegal. We're on public land. All archaeological sites and relics are protected by law. Second, pothunting, as it's called, destroys the evidence we were just talking about. And third, what pothunters are really doing is grave robbing. The bones they dig up are the remains of people who are somebody's ancestors. That's what the name Anasazi means—somebody's ancestors. They might be *my* ancestors. Who knows? How would you like it if I dug up your grandfather's grave so I could steal his gold wedding ring and sell it to a collector?"

"Ugh," Jessica said. "How gross!"

"It's the same thing," Carina said. "The only difference is that the people of all the villages around here have been dead a lot longer."

Alex shivered. "Can we talk about something else?" he asked. "I don't like to think about all those dead people buried around here. I mean, here we are, sitting around a campfire, miles from anybody, talking about ancient graves. All we need is some scary music to be in the opening scene of a thriller flick."

Frank glanced around. Night was falling fast, though a little light still lingered in the western sky. The rocks and trees took on strange shapes in the twilight.

Suddenly Lisa screamed. "Look!" she shouted. "Up there!"

Frank twisted around, then leapt to his feet. The moon was just rising over the edge of the bluff behind them. Silhouetted against the pale light was the unmistakable form of a man with a rifle in his hands!

53

6 Ambushed!

Mike jumped up. "Keep calm, everybody," he said firmly. "There's no danger. I'll handle this."

Joe got up and stood next to his brother, ready to give Mike a hand if it looked as if he needed it.

Mike walked away from the fire and cupped his hands around his mouth. "Hello up there," he called. "Is that you, Jake? Come on down and have a cup of coffee."

Up above, the man with the rifle disappeared from the skyline. A moment later, there was a little avalanche of pebbles as he scrambled down the hillside in their direction.

Joe thought that the man who stepped into the firelight looked as if he might have been wandering through the back country for a hundred years. His frayed overalls and flannel shirt were so faded that they were almost white. His raggedy shoulder-length hair and long full beard were almost white, too. On his head was a battered, sweat-stained felt hat. The lever-action Winchester rifle in his hands might have been even older than he was, but it was clearly well cared for.

From beneath bushy white eyebrows, the man's dark blue eyes studied the members of the group, who were all on their feet now, looking apprehensive. "I been watching you," he said, in a voice that was hoarse from lack of use.

"I know," Tom said. "I saw you this afternoon."

"Maybe you did and maybe you didn't," the man replied. "There's not many that spot old Jake when he don't want to be seen."

Mike stepped over to him. "How about that cup of coffee, Jake?" he said.

"Nope, no coffee. I just come down to give you a warning." He paused and gave the teens an eerie look. "Strangers ain't safe in these parts."

"I'm no stranger, Jake," Mike said. "You know that. I was born not a day's ride from here."

"No, you're no stranger, no more'n your Indian friend there." Jake nodded toward Tom. "But you been bringing strangers into the area, whole bunches of 'em. That's got to stop right now, you hear? If you got any sense, you'll clear out pronto, while you're still healthy," he added, waving his rifle.

Mike's fists clenched and his face became taut. He took a step forward. "Jake," he said in a quiet voice, "if I didn't know better, I'd say that sounded an awful lot like a threat. I'm not someone who likes threats any better than the next fellow."

Jake raised the barrel of his rifle an inch or two. Joe sensed menace in the gesture. He crouched slightly, ready to jump at the old man from the side if he pointed the gun at Mike or anyone else. Frank, on the man's other side, looked ready to spring, too.

"Take it any way you want," Jake said, lowering the barrel of the rifle toward the ground again. "But if you're smart, you'll turn around and go back to where you came from. I won't answer for the consequences if you don't."

From the background, Lisa was aiming her camera at the old man. He saw her and took a step in her direction, wearing an awful scowl. As she recoiled, Frank stepped between her and the prospector.

Jake looked back at Mike and said, "Heed what I say, if you know what's good for you." Then, before Mike could reply, he turned on his heel and walked away into the darkness. A couple of minutes later, the sound of hoofbeats reached the campfire.

"Whew!" Carina said, coming forward and wiping her forehead. "Was that guy for real?"

"Sort of," Mike said. "That was Jake Swenson, known around here as Crazy Jake, though nobody calls him that to his face. He's been roaming the area for twenty years or more, prospecting for uranium."

"He found it, too, or so he says," Tom added. "I think it's all in his head, but I've heard stories of

56

people getting shot at if they're too curious about a certain area not far from here."

Lisa looked at him with wide eyes. "He shoots at people, just because they're in the wrong place? That's crazy!"

From the other side of the campfire, Billy Bob let out a loud laugh. "Yup," he said. "That's why folks call him Crazy Jake."

Lisa turned back to Mike. "Can't you do something about the old guy?" she asked. "Nobody told me we might get shot at on this trip."

"I don't think there's any danger," Mike began.

Jessica, who was standing a few steps apart from the others, loudly interrupted. "Of course there's no danger. At least, not from that ham who just left. Listen, Mike, you really need a new scriptwriter. That 'Clear out while you're still healthy' bit is from, like, caveman times."

Joe scanned her face. "Jessica," he said, "are you suggesting that Crazy Jake isn't the real thing?"

"Of course he isn't the real thing!"

"Why do you think that?" Frank said.

"Oh, come on," she replied, rolling her eyes. "Weird threats from an old prospector? Give me a break! Mike obviously got him from central casting, rented him a wig and a fake beard, and told him to give us a scare. He must have figured out that this tour of his needed a little extra atmosphere. And all you nerds fell for it, too. Not me."

"Now, why is it," Greg said, as if thinking aloud,

"that total phonies always think everyone else is a phony, too?"

"Go crawl back into that Louisiana swamp you came from," Jessica replied hotly.

"Now, just hold it, all of you!" Mike stepped into the firelight with his arms spread wide, palms down. "One of the first rules on a trail ride is that everybody has to get along. *Has* to, you hear? We depend on each other. We don't all have to be good friends, but no quarrels and no feuds. Is that clear?"

"Sure, Mike," Greg said, looking down and drawing a line in the dirt with the toe of his boot. "I'm sorry."

"Forget it, Greg," Mike replied. "Jessica? What about you?"

For a moment, Jessica looked stubborn. Then she sighed loudly and said in an overly sweet voice, "Oh, for sure. Let's all make friends."

Joe thought she sounded about as convincing as a used-car salesman.

Mike turned away from Jessica and said, "Greg, a little bird tells me that you've got a surprise for everybody in your pack. How about giving us a tune or two?"

Greg, flushing with pleasure, said, "You bet, Mike." He went off in the direction of the chuck wagon and returned a few moments later with a small red accordion.

"I'm going to play a two-step, a kind of dance tune, called 'Adieu, Michele,'" he announced. Then he launched into a tune with so much rhythm and bounce that Joe had trouble standing still. Soon everyone was clapping in time.

"Who wants to learn the two-step?" Carina called over the music. Nick, red-faced, got up and joined her. Soon they were dancing around the fire.

When the tune ended, Lisa said, "That was terrific, Greg. But why don't you have any keys on your accordion? I have a cousin who plays accordion, and his has a whole row of keys down one side, just like a piano."

"That's what's called a piano-accordion. This is a button accordion," he replied, holding it up for her to see. "It's used all the time in traditional Cajun music. Cajuns are the French-speaking people in Louisiana," he added, as he began to play another bouncy tune.

After three tunes, Mike asked, "Do you know anything we could sing along with?" Mike threw a log on the fire, and Joe watched the neon orange sparks fly upward and disappear.

Greg thought for a moment, then said, "How about 'On Top of Old Smoky'?"

As Greg played the first notes of a lead-in, Joe overheard Jessica mutter, "Bo-ring!" He was glad she had enough sense not to say it too loudly.

Joe and Frank were sharing a pup tent. During the night, Joe opened his eyes, suddenly alert. What had awakened him?

He lay still and listened. He could hear Frank

breathing in the sleeping bag next to him. Outside the tent, a light breeze was rustling the leaves of the trees, but he thought he heard a more regular sound as well, like stealthy footsteps. They came closer, then receded. Someone was creeping around the camp!

He rolled over onto his stomach, propped himself on his elbows, and looked out through the open flaps of the tent. The moonlight made the clearing look as if it were drawn in smudgy blue crayon on gray paper. Now and then, the breeze made some of the banked coals from the campfire wink orange.

Moving as quietly as he could, Joe wriggled out of his sleeping bag and groped around for his jeans, sweatshirt, and shoes. Once dressed, he cautiously unzipped the screen door of the tent and stepped outside. The night air was chilly on his face.

He took a slow, careful look around. The moon seemed to cast more shadows than light. When he looked up toward the sky, he thought he saw the form of someone sitting atop the nearby bluff. Jake, keeping an eye on them? A moment later, the form was gone—or had he imagined it?

On the far side of the camp, one of the horses gave a low nicker. What had disturbed it? Joe wondered. The figure from the bluff? The intruder he'd heard earlier? Or were they the same person?

Walking on tiptoe, Joe started toward the horses. Part of his attention went to avoiding stepping on a stick or leaf that might make a noise and betray his presence to the prowler—or prowlers. The rest was focused on looking and listening for anything that seemed out of place.

But he wasn't alert enough. Behind him there was a faint sound of a footstep on sandy ground. Then, a split-second later, an arm slipped around his neck and tightened in a deadly choke hold!

7 A Traitor in the Midst

The arm tightened around Joe's throat. He grabbed it with both hands and tried to pull it away, but he didn't have the leverage he needed. He gasped for air. His attacker's breath rasped in his left ear. Joe tried kicking backward, but his heel hit nothing.

Still holding his attacker's arm, Joe bent his knees and lunged forward, as if trying for a shoulder throw. The attacker reacted by pulling back. Instantly Joe shifted direction and threw all his weight backward, thrusting with his bent legs. Overbalanced, the other guy fell back, with Joe on top of him. As they hit the ground, Joe grasped his right fist in his left hand, twisted at the waist, and put everything he had into a backward elbow thrust to the midsection.

"Unnnh!" Air whooshed out of his attacker's lungs. The arm around Joe's throat loosened for a moment. Instantly Joe pulled free, rolled over, and kneeled on his opponent's chest. Grabbing him by the shirtfront, he cocked his fist for a blow that would finish the battle.

The moon came out from behind a cloud. The pale light struck his opponent's face.

"Billy Bob!" Joe exclaimed. He kept his voice low. There was no point in waking the whole camp. "What—!" He released the chuck wagon driver and jumped to his feet.

"Joe? Is that you?" Billy Bob asked groggily. He pushed himself up to a sitting position and rubbed his stomach.

"Why did you jump me?" Joe demanded in a loud whisper.

"I heard somebody prowling around the campsite," the chuck wagon driver said. He sounded as if he was in pain. "When I got up to look, I saw you sneaking off in the direction of the horses. So I went after you. What were you doing, anyway?"

"I heard a prowler, too," Joe replied. "Over near the horses. I was trying to creep up on whoever it was when you started choking me."

"Sorry, my mistake," Billy Bob said. "Are you okay?"

Joe felt his throat. It was bruised, but he'd be all right. "Yeah. How about you?"

Billy Bob got to his feet and slowly straightened up.

He pressed against his rib cage. "Nothing broken, I guess," he said. "You gotta lighten up on those punches."

"Couldn't you see who I was?" Joe demanded.

"Not in this light. Anyway, a prowler's a prowler. Boy, you sure hit me a pretty good one."

"I was in a hurry to start breathing again," Joe explained.

"You say you heard somebody near the horses?" Billy Bob asked.

Joe nodded. "I thought I did. But even if somebody was there, the noise we made probably scared him off."

Billy Bob looked in that direction. "I reckon I ought to check," he said.

"I'll come with you."

But when they reached the area where the horses were tethered, there was nothing to see. Joe's white horse stood out brightly in the moonlight. It neighed softly when he patted its nose. The other horses were all calm.

"You better get some sleep," Billy Bob finally told Joe. "We've got a long day on the trail ahead of us."

"Good idea," Joe replied, yawning. "I'll see you in the morning."

The first rays of sun arrowed through the open tent flaps, straight at Frank's face. He flung his arm over his eyes and tried to go back to sleep. Outside, others were stirring. He heard low voices talking, right next to the side of the tent.

"It's just a five-minute walk from here," the first voice said. It sounded like Alex. "You'll pick up a path that leads right to it."

The other voice belonged to Lisa. "I don't know," she said. "This early morning light really shows up the details, but maybe I should wait and see where we stop tonight. Evening light would work for the kinds of shots I'd want to take."

"You can wait if you want," Alex replied. "But our route won't take us past any villages as well preserved as the one near here. This may be your best chance to get the pictures you want."

"Yeah . . . I'll think about it," Lisa said.

As the voices faded, Frank yawned and stretched, then reached for his clothes. As he pulled on his boots, he found himself wondering how Alex knew so much about the territory they were going to be riding through. Wasn't he from St. Louis? Maybe he was one of those guys who love to study maps and guides and ended up knowing more about an area than people who had lived there all their lives.

Joe was still asleep. Frank leaned over, shook his shoulder, and said, "Let's go, little bro. Rise and shine."

An instant later, Frank was flat on his back, with Joe's hands reaching for his neck. Frank pushed his arms up and thrust outward, breaking Joe's hold, and said, "Hey, whoa there! I'm Frank Hardy, remember? Your brother. What's wrong with you?"

Joe blinked and took a deep breath, then rubbed his

face. "Oh. Sorry, Frank," he said. "I had a hard night."

As the Hardys dressed, Joe told Frank about his encounter with Billy Bob.

When Joe was finished, Frank asked, "Any sign of the intruder? Any idea what he was up to?"

Joe shook his head. "No, to both questions. It could have been Jake, I guess. I thought I saw someone up on the bluff."

Frank nodded thoughtfully. "And don't forget Ramirez. He might have come sneaking around after we all went to sleep."

"True. For that matter, it could have been Billy Bob, pulling a fast one on me," Joe replied. "Whoever it was, I have a hunch we'd better keep our eyes open for nasty surprises. Also, I'd better tell Mike about last night, first thing."

Outside, a faint *ding!* was immediately followed by a deafening clamor. Frank dashed out of the tent, with Joe right behind him. In the middle of the camp, next to the campfire, Billy Bob was banging on his iron triangle, calling the group to breakfast.

A line of sleepy-looking people formed next to the chuck wagon for plates of bacon, scrambled eggs, and home-fried potatoes. Billy Bob looked down the line and said, "We're short one, Mike. Lisa must still be asleep."

"She can't be," Mike replied. "I saw her earlier this morning. She took some pictures while I was building the campfire."

Billy Bob looked around again. "Well, she's not

here now. She didn't get any breakfast, and it's going to be a long time till lunch."

"Um . . ." Alex said hesitantly. "She might have gone to take pictures of the ruins."

"All alone?" Mike demanded. "Why would she do a silly thing like that? We could have all gone after breakfast."

"Well . . . I told her the ruins were pretty special, and she said that early morning light is the best for the kinds of pictures she wanted to take."

Mike glanced around grimly. "Tom, will you take a look? She's probably okay, but—"

"I'll come along," Frank offered. He grabbed two pieces of bacon and a piece of toast off his plate. "You may need help."

Joe was right behind him.

A well-worn trail led up the hillside. Tom paused at one point and indicated a mark in the dust. "She came this way, all right," he said.

On the other side of the hill, in a hollow, was a collection of low stone walls that looked more like a maze than the remains of a village. Tom cupped his hands and shouted, "Lisa?"

"Over here," her voice replied weakly. "I can't move!"

Tom and Frank hurried down to the ruins and followed the sound of Lisa's voice. She was lying in one of the walled-off areas. Her foot had apparently slipped into a crevice between two large stones, catching her by the ankle. Her face was pale, and there were tear tracks on her dirty cheeks.

"Boy, am I glad to see you! I tried to get loose, but those rocks were too heavy for me to move," she told them, showing a scratched and bleeding hand.

"How about your leg?" Tom asked. "Does it feel like anything's broken?"

"No, no, it's fine. Just stuck, that's all."

"Frank? Joe?" Tom said. Frank bent down and got a solid grip on one of the stones, while Tom and Joe grabbed the other. Tom said, "On three. One, two . . ."

Frank took a deep breath, braced himself, and pulled. The heavy stone resisted, then came away so suddenly that he had to skip backward so it wouldn't land on his foot.

"Oof! That feels a lot better," Lisa said. She pushed herself to her feet, with a helping hand from Tom, then bent down to pick up her camera. "I hope nothing broke," she added. "I was getting some incredible shots before I got stuck."

She was limping a little, so Joe offered her his elbow.

Back at camp, Lisa listened meekly while Mike told her, in front of everyone, never to go off exploring on her own.

"Those ruins can be dangerous if you don't know your way around," he said. "Some of them have underground chambers called kivas. You could have fallen into one, or tangled with a rattlesnake. The next time you want to go somewhere or see something, let one of us know. We'll do our best to arrange it."

He looked around the circle of listeners and added,

"That goes for all of you. Okay?" Everyone nodded. "Fine. Then let's break camp and hit the trail. Today's ride is going to take us through some of the most beautiful country in the West."

Frank and Joe struck their tent, tossed it and their packs in the chuck wagon, and went over to saddle their horses. The others in the group were busy doing the same.

Jessica's horse was tied up next to Frank's. He watched as she lifted the saddle onto her horse's back and cinched the strap.

Remembering her accident of the day before, Frank asked, "Would you like me to check the strap for you, to make sure it's tight enough?"

She gave him a cold look. "I've been riding since I was three years old," she said. "I can take care of it myself."

Frank shrugged. "Sure, whatever you say."

Jessica turned her back to them. Putting her foot in the stirrup, she vaulted up into the saddle. As Frank watched, she vaulted past the saddle and tumbled to the ground on the other side of her horse.

There was a short, shocked silence. Mike hurried over to see what had happened. When Jessica stood up, mad enough to spit but obviously not hurt, everyone broke out laughing. Frank couldn't help joining in. She had looked exactly like an actress in a slapstick comedy.

"Okay, who's the clown?" Jessica demanded loudly.

Greg stopped laughing long enough to choke out

the words, "You are! Could you wait until somebody gets a camcorder, then do that bit again? It would definitely win a contest for funny home videos."

Jessica scowled and brushed off her jeans. "Somebody monkeyed with my stirrup," she announced. "It's much too high now. That's why I missed the saddle and fell off on the other side."

Frank, followed by Joe, went over to look at the left stirrup. Jessica was right—it was much higher than the one on the other side.

"Didn't you notice it was higher when you put your foot in it?" Joe asked.

"No. I was thinking about something else," she replied. "So who's the joker? Who's been messing with the saddles?"

No one spoke. Finally Tom said, "Last night I threw a tarp over all the saddles, to protect them from the dew. But I didn't touch your stirrup strap, Jessica. Besides, anybody who knew the number on your saddle could have hunted it up and fiddled with it."

"Pretty risky," Joe commented. "Somebody might have noticed."

"*I* noticed!" Jessica proclaimed. She turned and pointed an accusing finger at Nick. "You sneaked over here last night after supper. Don't try to deny it. I saw you!"

"Is this true, Nick?" Mike asked.

"What, that I came over here after supper?" Nick replied, brushing his dark hair out of his eyes. "Yes, it is. So what? I wasn't doing anything to her dumb saddle."

70

"Then what were you doing?" Mike continued.

To Frank, the boy from New York City looked both embarrassed and defiant. "I came over to give Cinnamon a piece of carrot," Nick told Tom. "I guess I should have asked you if it was okay, but . . . well, she's a really neat horse, and I thought she deserved a little treat."

"And that's all?" Mike asked. "You didn't touch the saddle?"

"I swear I didn't," Nick replied, drawing an X on his chest.

Mike glanced over at Frank and raised a questioning eyebrow. In reply, Frank gave a little sideways shake of his head. He didn't think there was much to be gained from further questioning at this point. And besides, Nick seemed to be telling the truth.

"Tom, will you adjust Jessica's stirrup for her?" Mike said. "The rest of you, finish packing your gear and getting ready. We hit the trail in five minutes."

Alex was standing next to Frank. "Five minutes?" he repeated in dismay. "I'm still taking my tent down. I'll never be ready in time."

"I'll come give you a hand as soon as I finish saddling Star," Frank offered.

"Great," Alex said. "I'll go get started."

As he walked away, Frank wondered about him. If Joe had really heard a prowler during the night, it might have been Jake or Ramirez or Billy Bob, but it might also have been one of the teens. And Alex was the only one who had a tent to himself. It would have been much easier for him to sneak out than for anyone

71

else. Frank decided that he and Joe needed to find time to sit down with Mike and go over the case so far.

A couple of minutes later, Frank went over to help Alex. The lanky, sandy-haired boy was squatting next to his collapsed tent, tossing crumbs to a couple of chipmunks, who scampered away at Frank's approach.

"Cute, aren't they?" Alex said. "This is such a great area for watching wildlife. One time I saw a fight between a rattlesnake and a roadrunner. It was pretty grim, but exciting, too. I couldn't help cheering when the bird won."

"That must have been something to see," Frank said. "When was this? The other day, before Joe and I got here?"

"Uh, no, it—uh-oh, I'd better hurry up with this stuff. I don't want Mike to leave me behind." He turned away from Frank and started rolling the tent.

Frank studied his back for a couple of seconds. Alex was obviously trying to hide the fact that he knew this area well. Why?

Alex's pack was on the ground, unzipped. Frank picked it up and said, "I'll take your gear to the chuck wagon."

"Thanks," Alex said without turning.

As he walked across the campsite, Frank quickly rifled the contents of the pack. Nothing out of the ordinary, except . . . Near the bottom of the pack, his fingers touched something hard wrapped up in a T-shirt.

He pulled it out for a look. It was a rolled-up

western belt with a design of leaves, flowers, and deer heads tooled into the leather. On the big engraved buckle was a picture of a jeep with a cloud of dust behind it and mountains in the background. Across the bottom, in fancy script, were the letters ORA.

Frank stared at the buckle. ORA . . . Off-Road Adventures! Alex was connected with Roy Ramirez, Mike's rival. And Ramirez had every reason to want to destroy Teen Trails West!

8 Out of Control

As the group hit the trail, Frank motioned to Joe to stay at the back of the line. He told him about Alex's belt buckle.

Joe whistled softly. "So Alex is connected with Ramirez and his outfit. That explains how he knows so much about the area. It also makes him our top suspect for sabotage. All we have to do now is keep an eye on him and catch him in the act."

When Frank didn't respond, Joe gave him a sharp look. "Well?" he added. "You agree, don't you?"

"About Alex? I guess so. It's pretty obvious." He pulled a red bandanna from his hip pocket and took off his hat to wipe his forehead. "Whew! It's hot in the sun, isn't it?"

"What do you mean, you *guess* so?" Joe demanded.

Frank tilted his head to one side and said, "Don't you get the feeling that Alex is a little *too* obvious a suspect? If I were pulling dirty tricks, I'd do my best to hide my connection to the people I was pulling them for. What would it cost me to leave a fancy belt at home?"

Joe gave a snort. "Sometimes I think you'd like it better if all the bad guys were criminal masterminds. But most bad guys make dumb mistakes. Alex's keeping that belt in his pack ranks as a dumb mistake."

"You're right," Frank said. "And we'll watch him like one of those hawks we saw a little while ago. But think about this. Two of the acts of sabotage were aimed at Jessica. Why her?"

Joe laughed. "That's easy. She's a royal pain in the neck." The path narrowed, and Joe had to duck to avoid a low-hanging branch. Behind him, Frank did the same.

"I'm with you there," Frank said. "But if Alex is working with Ramirez, trying to ruin Teen Trails, wouldn't he see to it that lots of people on the tour had accidents? Why just one of us?"

"But it's not just one of us," Joe pointed out. "What about the baggage that was mysteriously left behind? And the pins in the saddle blankets? Those were aimed at other people—me, for one. And Alex had as good a chance as anyone to pull those off."

"Okay, okay," Frank said, nudging his horse to move up to Joe's side. "But what's Alex's motive in all this? Oh, and don't forget there were accidents on earlier tours, too. Alex wasn't along then. Does that

75

mean that Ramirez had another inside person on those? Our theory is starting to get a little too complicated, if you ask me."

"How about this?" Joe suggested. "Remember the earlier incidents—Lorna, the daughter of the talk show host, falling in a thorn bush and all? Maybe they really were accidents, but they gave Ramirez the idea of sending Alex on this tour and setting up a few more."

"Not bad," Frank replied. "But do me a favor. Don't cross anyone else off your list yet."

"I won't," Joe promised. "And to prove that I mean it, I think we ought to separate and mingle with the others. Someone might have noticed some clue or evidence we missed. Besides, Alex might not be working alone."

Frank nodded. "Deal. We can compare notes at lunch. And we can tell Mike about the buckle then."

Frank urged Star into a faster walk that brought him alongside Carina. Joe stayed at the tail of the line for a few moments, wondering whom he should start with. Lisa? She had been on the tour before. That gave her a better opportunity than the others. She had been the victim of an accident that morning, but hers really did seem to be her own fault. But as he was about to join her, she moved up next to Tom and started talking to him. Joe decided to wait to get her alone.

About thirty feet ahead, Greg and Nick were riding side by side. The trail was plenty wide enough for a third rider. Joe decided to join them.

When Joe cantered Magic up to them, Nick was talking about tarantulas. "It's just pure prejudice," he was saying. "Okay, so they're big and hairy, and they have long legs and run fast. So? They won't hurt you. Everybody's scared of them because they think they're poisonous, but they're not really."

"Do tarantulas live around here?" Greg asked Nick. He cast a wicked glance at Jessica, who was riding a short distance ahead of them. "Maybe we could catch one and slip it into you-know-who's tent tonight."

"I don't think so," Nick said. "You have to go to places like South Texas to find tarantulas. I trapped a really neat cricket this morning, though." He gave Joe a friendly glance. "Did you know that they sing by rubbing their hind legs together?"

"That's news to me," Joe replied.

Greg said, "Can I borrow that cricket tonight? It might do just as good a job as a spider."

"Sorry, I let it go," Nick replied. "You should have seen the jump it made when I dumped it out of the collecting jar. Five feet, at least!"

"Neat," Greg said. "I wish I was back home in Louisiana—I'd go out to the ditch and find me a crawdad and put it in her sleeping bag!"

"I can't imagine who you guys are talking about," Joe said lightly. "But the next time somebody messes with her saddle, I'll know who to suspect."

"Hey, wait a minute," Greg protested. "A joke's one thing, but loosening a saddle is different. Somebody might've gotten really hurt."

Nick looked troubled. "I don't know, Greg," he said. "Is it so different? What if you put a spider in her tent, and when she saw it, she jumped up and hit her head on the tent pole, then she tripped over something and sprained her ankle?"

Greg grinned. "Leave out the sprained ankle, and I'd say, Let's do it! Anyway, there *is* a difference. If you loosen somebody's saddle, they're almost bound to be hurt. The only question is how bad. But with a spider in your tent or an ice cube down your neck, chances are you won't get hurt. If you do, it's just bad luck."

"But it's still the fault of the guy who pulls the joke," Nick said.

"Jessica isn't the only one who's had weird accidents," Joe pointed out. "What about those pins in my saddle blanket yesterday?"

Greg shrugged. "There wasn't anything funny about that. Tom forgot to take them out, that's all."

"How about all the gear that got left behind?" Nick demanded.

"That wasn't a joke, either," Greg replied. "Billy Bob probably took the stuff out of the wagon to make room for some supplies he was loading, then forgot to put it back in. Anyway, what's your point?"

"I don't know," Nick admitted. "I just hope—" He caught his breath and exclaimed, "Look at that!"

"What?" Joe asked, twisting in his saddle. "What is it?"

Nick pointed toward the top of a tall, narrow pillar

of rock. "It's a bald eagle!" he replied. "I never dreamed we'd see one. The guidebook I read said that you mostly see them around here in the winter. I bet it's nesting on the cliff face."

Joe squinted upward. The bird that was making lazy circles near the top of the cliff was very big and dark, with what might be a white head, but Joe would have to take Nick's word that it was a bald eagle.

Mike, at the head of the column, had moved his horse off the trail and was speaking to all the riders as they passed him. Everyone turned to look up at the cliff.

"There's an eagle up there," Mike said as Joe, Greg, and Nick approached. The three reined in their horses next to him.

"We saw it," Nick said excitedly.

"Nick spotted it," Greg added.

"You've got good eyes," Mike said. "From now on, I'm going to keep my binoculars with me. I don't want to miss another chance like that. We'll be stopping for lunch in about half an hour."

"Oh, good," Nick said with a groan. "I don't know if I can take much more time in the saddle. My back's starting to hurt."

Mike gave him a sharp glance. "If you're serious, maybe you'd better spend the afternoon riding with Billy Bob in the chuck wagon. These problems clear up a lot faster when you catch them early."

They rode on. After a short silence, Nick said, "I think I really am getting a backache. If I have to ride

79

in the chuck wagon, would one of you come along? Billy Bob's okay, but I wouldn't know what to say to him."

Joe considered for a moment. Billy Bob was one of the people he wanted to talk to, and Nick's request gave him the perfect excuse. "Sure," Joe said. "I'll come along. Magic could probably use a little vacation from me, anyway."

After lunch, Joe gave his horse to Tom, who already had the reins of Nick's horse tied to his saddle horn.

Billy Bob and Nick had taken their places in the chuck wagon. There was just enough room for Joe on the right side. Grasping the iron post at the front of the wagon, he put his foot on the tiny step and pulled himself up onto the wooden seat. Then he wedged himself in and propped one foot up against the wooden splashboard that went across the width of the wagon, to protect the riders from flying mud.

"I feel as if I ought to be carrying a shotgun," Joe remarked. "Like in all the movies."

"There's a big difference between a chuck wagon and a Wells Fargo stagecoach," Billy Bob replied. "We're not carrying any passengers or gold, for one thing."

"And we've only got one horse," Nick said. "Though Pom-Pom looks big enough to count as two or three horses."

Billy Bob picked up the reins and reached down to release the hand brake. "Hang on, folks, here we go."

When he shook the reins, Pom-Pom leaned his weight forward against the horseshoe-shaped yoke around his neck. Then he started to walk, while the chuck wagon rolled along behind.

The biggest surprise for Joe was how much the wagon rocked from side to side. With every bump, he felt as though they were about to turn over. But after the first few minutes, he stopped clutching the armrest and bracing himself. He even started to enjoy the rhythmic motion.

"Why does Pom-Pom have that wide leather strap under his tail?" Nick asked.

"That's the back band," Billy Bob replied. "When we're moving, the horse pulls against the yoke, but when we slow down, he has to have some way to push back against the weight of the wagon."

They reached the top of a small rise. Billy Bob sat up a little straighter and tightened his grip on the reins.

"Hold on," he warned. "Pom-Pom has to speed up going downhill, to keep from being run over by the wagon."

As soon as the chuck wagon crested the rise and started down, Pom-Pom broke into a trot. Joe could see that the trail went straight for most of the downhill slope, then curved sharply to the left near the bottom.

Billy Bob put his right boot on the two-foot-long brake lever that protruded from the floorboards and set it a little tighter. The wagon was swaying even more. Nick grabbed Joe's arm and hung on tightly. With every uneven spot on the trail—and there were a lot of them—the creaky wagon bounced madly.

"Slow down!" Nick shouted, over the racket. "This isn't safe!"

Billy Bob didn't answer, but he pushed harder on the brake lever. For a moment, the wagon seemed to slow a little, then it picked up speed again. Billy Bob muttered something under his breath, pulled back on the reins, and shouted, "Whoa, Pom-Pom! Take it easy, big guy!"

Pom-Pom paid no attention. Billy Bob stood up, tugged harder on the reins, and put all the weight of his right foot on the brake lever.

Zing! There was a sharp report, almost like a gunshot. The brake lever swung loosely to the floorboards.

"No brakes!" Billy Bob yelled. He had been pushing hard against the brake lever. Deprived of its support, he staggered forward, flailed his arms wildly, and threw himself sideways to avoid going headfirst over the splashboard.

"Look out!" Nick screamed.

Joe leaned forward and reached across Nick to make a grab for Billy Bob's arm. But at that moment, Billy Bob, still falling sideways, caught his hip on the armrest of the seat. He gave a startled yell and tumbled over the side of the wagon. He had just enough time to throw the reins in Joe's direction.

Pom-Pom, frightened by the commotion, broke into a full gallop. As Joe grasped the reins, he saw that the bend in the trail was only a few dozen yards ahead. The chuck wagon was rolling out of control down the hill. It could never make it around the sharp curve without overturning!

9 Sniper Attack

Joe risked a quick glance at Nick. The boy's wide-eyed look of terror told Joe that he understood the danger they were in.

"Hang on with all you've got!" Joe shouted over the thunder of Pom-Pom's hooves and the rattle of the wagon wheels on the rock-strewn trail. "I'll try to stop this thing!"

Joe braced his shoulders against the back of the wagon seat, and one foot against the splashboard, wedging himself in to keep from being thrown from side to side. Then he tightened his grip on the reins, twisting one around each hand to make sure they didn't slip through his grasp, and slowly began to pull back on them.

"Whoa, Pom-Pom!" he yelled. "Whoa, boy, easy!"

The white horse's ears flicked around backward, and he tossed his head as if in answer to Joe's call. The rhythm of his hoofbeats changed; he seemed to be pushing against his back band.

"He's trying to slow us down!" Joe shouted to Nick. "But I don't think he can do it!"

"We'll never make it around the curve!" Nick shouted back. "Should we jump off the wagon?"

Joe shook his head. "If you fell under the wheels, you'd be killed for sure! I'll keep trying to stop us!" He kept the pressure on the reins, but he was starting to believe that the situation was hopeless. In another moment, the chuck wagon was sure to crash.

"What in the world does Billy Bob think he's up to?" Frank asked Mike, who was riding next to him some distance ahead of the others. They had been discussing the case. "Look how fast he's going—he'll turn over if he doesn't slow down!"

The top-heavy chuck wagon was speeding up, rocking wildly from side to side. When one of the wheels hit a big rock, it bounced so high that Frank could see daylight under it.

"Something's wrong!" Mike said urgently. "Come on, we've got to help stop that wagon!" He spurred his horse into a gallop.

Frank was close behind him. He had to concentrate on staying in the saddle, but he still had room in his mind to wonder just *how* Mike planned to stop the runaway wagon. It looked like an impossible job.

As they neared the back of the wagon, Mike

shouted, "Go left! Get your rope onto something solid!"

Frank saw that Mike was unlimbering the lasso strapped to the side of his saddle. He glanced down at the rope on his own saddle and started unstrapping it.

Mike's horse was alongside the rear of the chuck wagon now, but Star, forced to gallop along the edge of the trail, was having trouble gaining ground. Frank unbuckled the strap of his lasso and took it in his free hand. As he had hoped, one end formed a loop.

Star was gaining on the wagon. The driver's seat was only a few feet ahead now. In the front corner of the chuck wagon Frank saw a thick iron rod that stuck up in the air. It looked strong enough to take the strain . . . *if* Frank could drop the loop of his rope over it and then hold on to it.

He saw that he was now in a better position to pull off the rescue than Mike. It was up to him.

Nick turned around, and Frank caught sight of him, white-faced and clinging to the edge of the seat with both hands.

"You'll be okay!" Frank shouted. He wished he felt as confident as he was trying to sound.

"Hurry!" Nick shouted back. "Hurry!"

Frank shook out more rope and looped it twice around the saddle horn. As Star came even with the seat of the wagon, Frank stood up in the stirrups and leaned forward to toss the noose over the iron rod on the chuck wagon. He caught just a second's glimpse of his brother, jaws clenched grimly, wrestling with the reins. Then Star, true to his cow pony training, dug in his hooves and threw his weight backward against the strain on the rope.

The rope hissed around the saddle horn, sending up a little puff of acrid gray smoke. Frank pulled hard at the other end, to tighten the coils that encircled the saddle horn and increase the friction on the rope. Then he had to give it a little slack when Star threatened to stumble.

The wagon was slowing down. The tight curve lay just ahead, and Frank didn't think the wagon could get around safely. He leaned back in the saddle, tightened the rope a second time, and pulled back on the reins at the same moment. Once again, Star dug his hooves into the soft earth, throwing up a dense cloud of reddish dust that got in Frank's eyes and nose. He couldn't see, but he was aware that Star had come to a halt. And that meant the chuck wagon had, too.

Frank blinked and took a deep breath that was meant to end in a sigh of relief, but the dust set off a coughing fit. Tears filled his eyes. When he wiped them away, he saw that the wagon was only a few feet from the dangerous curve. Pom-Pom was bending his head down to munch at a clump of grass.

Joe jumped down from the chuck wagon seat and ran over to Frank. Nick was right behind him.

"Neat rescue, bro," Joe called, grinning. "That was really exciting, but next time I think I'll stay home and watch it on the tube."

"I don't blame you," Frank replied. He gave Star a pat on the neck, then climbed down. "What happened?"

"I'd like to know the answer to that myself," Joe said. "We started down the hill, and Billy Bob tried to slow us down, but the brakes failed. Then Billy Bob fell off the wagon. Is he okay?"

Frank shook his head. "I don't know."

He glanced over his shoulder. Mike was riding back up the trail. Billy Bob was limping down to meet him. The rest of the group had stopped at the top of the rise and was watching the scene anxiously.

"I think Billy Bob's okay," Frank said. "How about you guys?"

"I'm all right," Nick said, though his voice trembled a little. "Wait till I tell my friends back on the Upper West Side that I was aboard a runaway chuck wagon. They'll think I'm the biggest liar they ever met!"

"I'm not hurt," Joe said. "But I'd sure like to know what caused that." He got down on his hands and knees and peered at the underside of the wagon, just behind the front wheels.

After a moment, he exclaimed, "There's the problem. The brake cable broke. It couldn't take the strain."

Frank joined him under the wagon. The cable of woven wire led back from the underside of the brake lever to a yoke, then divided to run to the brakes on the two rear wheels. It had snapped just ahead of the yoke.

"Funny," Frank said, reaching for one of the dangling ends. "These cables are rated for five or ten times the tension they're likely to meet . . . Joe, look at this! The broken wires on the lower part of the cable are jagged, but the upper ones broke perfectly evenly. What does that tell you?"

Joe took the wire, peered at it, and said, "Our near-accident wasn't accidental. Somebody cut the cable halfway through, knowing it would snap the first time it was put under a lot of tension."

"Hey, what are you doing under there?" Mike said, stooping by the side of the chuck wagon to peer at them. Frank showed him the cable and explained.

Mike's expression grew grim. "Billy Bob got off with a few scratches, but he could have been badly hurt," he said. "And Nick and Joe were nearly killed. Who would be cold-blooded enough to do this?"

"Somebody who's determined to drive you out of business," Joe replied.

Mike shook his head slowly. "One more incident like this, and he or she might get his wish," he said. "It's not worth putting kids in danger, just to keep Teen Trails going."

"This isn't a time to make any big decisions," Frank advised. He scrambled out from under the wagon and straightened up. "Do you have what you need to fix the chuck wagon brakes, so the tour can continue?"

"We should. Billy Bob will know." He looked around. "We'd better camp here tonight. It's an okay spot, and we won't be that far off schedule."

* * *

89

While Billy Bob got to work on the chuck wagon, Mike insisted on taking everyone else on a hike, as a way of calming them down. Joe and Frank wanted to spend the time questioning people about who had been seen near the chuck wagon, but Mike refused to let them.

"I know somebody here's a bad guy," he told Joe and Frank. "But I'm going to do my best to give the rest of them what they came for."

Joe and Frank protested, but in the end, they gave in to Mike's plan. After all, he was calling the shots.

In the course of an hour's walk, the group saw jackrabbits, an elk, several red-tailed hawks, and a fast-moving sandy-colored blur that Mike said was a bobcat. Tom pointed out the wildflowers of the region, with names like pincushion, borrobush, and desert tobacco, which had long, slender white flowers and a heavy scent.

As they were walking along the crest of a bluff, Carina said, "Look, down there—aren't those lines in the ground? I can see straight lines and circles."

Tom nodded. "You're probably looking at a buried Anasazi village. The lines are the walls of houses, and the circles are kivas, the underground chambers that were like the churches of the Anasazi."

"We can see it, just like that?" Greg asked.

"Yes, because we are well above it," Tom replied. "If we were down there, we might walk right over it and not notice anything. These days, many archaeologists use photos from satellites to find ancient ruins that go unobserved by those on the ground."

Joe was looking in the other direction. "Mike?" he said in an undertone. "Can I borrow your binoculars?"

Mike passed them over, and Joe looked through them at the cloud of dust he had noticed across the valley. As he turned the focusing knob, an open jeep with a heavy roll bar sprang into view at the foot of a mesa. The dust that covered it made it impossible to tell if it was dark green or black, but he could see some letters on the door. Two men in western hats sat in front, with what looked like a pile of tools in the back.

The jeep disappeared around a bend. Joe told Frank and Mike what he had seen. "I wonder if that jeep's been shadowing us," he mused. "I think I know what it said on the door—ORA."

Frank gave a thoughtful nod. "If Alex is working for Ramirez, maybe he meets him now and then to report and get his orders. I wonder if anyone noticed Alex near the chuck wagon during the lunch break."

Later, back at camp, Frank grabbed Joe by the elbow and took him to one side.

"Bingo," Frank said. "After lunch, Alex got Lisa into a game of Frisbee. He kept making wild throws, then retrieving them himself. Twice he threw it under the chuck wagon, and both times Lisa thought it took him forever to get it back."

"Great cover story," Joe said. "Do we confront him about it?"

Frank shook his head. "He'd just deny it, and then he'd know that we're on to him. Let him get overconfident and he's more likely to make a mistake we can use to nail him."

Dinner that night was hamburgers and hot dogs, grilled over a fire of mesquite twigs. It was delicious. Joe went back for a second burger, then sat down again next to Alex.

"Great dinner, huh?" he said.

Alex looked at him blankly. "Oh . . . yeah, great," he replied. "Mesquite makes everything taste better, even toast."

"I don't remember having toast grilled over mesquite," Joe said. "When was that?"

"Uh . . . maybe I imagined it," Alex said, looking away. "I wonder what's for dessert."

On cue, Billy Bob appeared carrying a huge skillet. "For dessert," he announced, "we have a specialty of the house called apple-raisin duff."

The aroma from the skillet was enough to draw a round of applause. Billy Bob served up the pielike creation and went back to the chuck wagon to clear up.

After dessert, Tom threw more logs on the fire, and Greg took out his accordion. The sun was below the horizon, but the clouds in the west glowed orange. Overhead, the sky was a deep blue, almost black, sprinkled here and there with the first faint glimmers of stars.

"This is an Irish tune, called 'Lark in the Morning,'" Greg announced. He glanced down to check the position of his fingers on the buttons. But before he could start to play, the silence was shattered by the nearby sound of three closely spaced gunshots!

10 Running Dry

"Everybody down!" Frank shouted.

Even as he said it, Billy Bob was racing across the campsite. He circled around the chuck wagon and started to scramble up the hillside just beyond.

"Billy Bob! Wait! Be careful!" Mike shouted. He, too, started toward the source of the gunshots, with Frank, Joe, and Tom right behind him.

"No, don't go!" Jessica screamed. "We'll all be killed!"

Mike spun on his heels. "Everybody, get out of the firelight and stay calm," he said firmly. "We'll take care of the problem. It's probably just old Jake trying to put a scare into us."

Frank didn't wait to see if the members of the group took Mike's advice. He reached the foot of the hill and began to climb as quickly as he could, pulling himself up with the help of bushes and rocks. There was no time to lose. Billy Bob was already nearly to the top, all alone. If whoever fired the shots was still there, the chuck wagon driver might be in terrible danger.

As Frank neared the top, Billy Bob appeared in a narrow gap between two boulders.

"He disappeared," Billy Bob called to Frank and the others. "But this is where he was hiding, all right. I just spotted this on the ground."

Billy Bob held up something small that glittered in the fading light. When Frank got closer, he saw that it was a spent rifle shell.

"It's from a thirty-thirty," Billy Bob continued. "But that's no surprise. Around here, those guns are thicker than fleas on a junkyard dog."

Frank took a moment to catch his breath after the dash up the hill. Then he joined Billy Bob in the spot he had found. The narrow gap was perfect for an ambush—hidden and protected by the rocks on either side, but with a clear view of the camp below.

Frank gazed at the camp for a moment, then looked back at the space between the rocks. It was deeply shadowed now, almost black. Billy Bob must have really sharp eyes to have spotted that cartridge, Frank thought.

Joe, next to Frank, said in an undertone, "I checked my memory, and everybody was sitting around the fire when we heard those shots, including you-know-who."

"We'll talk later, after we look over the scene," Frank replied softly. Aloud he said, "Did anybody bring a flashlight?"

"Here," Tom said, producing a big flash from his hip pocket. He turned it on and aimed the beam into the sniper's hiding place.

"Here's another rifle shell," Frank said, bending down to pick it up.

"Careful, it might still be hot," Mike warned.

Frank touched it quickly with one fingertip, then picked it up. "Nope, it's already cooled off," he reported. "And here's number three."

"They've already cooled off?" Joe said. "That's weird."

Tom was squatting down on his heels, holding the light so it shone sideways over the dirt. "The ground's too scuffed up to see any prints," he said. "I reckon that varmint did it on purpose, to hide his tracks."

Joe turned to Frank and whispered, "That's a little too sensible for Crazy Jake, isn't it?"

They continued to search the area for a few minutes, but Frank did it without much hope. By now the night had fallen for real. Even with the help of Tom's flash, the chances were that they would walk right by any evidence the sniper had left behind.

"We'd better get back," Mike said suddenly. "Come on, Tom, Billy Bob. The kids must be having fits by now. Getting shot at is a little more wild West than they were bargaining for. We're going to have a job calming them down."

While the others hurried back to the campfire,

Frank and Joe hung back. "Well?" Frank began. "Any ideas?"

Joe rubbed his chin. "A few," he said. "Those shots were just meant to scare us. At such close range, anyone who's handy with a rifle could have hit anything he wanted to."

"I'll buy that," Frank said. "What else?"

"Well, obviously no one in the group did the shooting, because we were all sitting around the fire when it happened. But that doesn't help much. We already figured that he—or she—was probably working with somebody on the outside. Now we know it for sure."

Frank paused for a moment to put his thoughts in order, then said, "I'm not so sure we do. Look—I'm pretty certain that somebody in the group messed with Jessica's saddle. And the chuck wagon brakes *could* have been sabotaged days ago, before our bunch arrived, but it's more likely that it was done more recently, maybe by that prowler you heard last night. Was that a group member? Maybe, maybe not. The same with the pins in the saddle blankets. An outsider could have done it, but it would have been easier from the inside."

"Okay, but what's your point?" Joe demanded.

Frank frowned. "Just this—we know that Alex has a connection with Ramirez, who may be out to ruin Mike's business. And we saw a jeep earlier today that might belong to Ramirez. The logical conclusion would be that Alex is the saboteur, and Ramirez sneaked up and fired those shots. Right?"

Joe nodded. "It makes sense."

"But," Frank continued, "those shots were fired from a thirty-thirty. Who do we know who carries a thirty-thirty, who warned us that we'd be in danger if we hung around here, who's said to have taken shots at other people in this area, and who certainly doesn't seem to be playing with a full deck?"

"You agree with Mike that it was Crazy Jake up there?" Joe asked.

Frank hesitated. "Actually, I've changed my mind," he said finally. "I don't think Jake fired those shots. Sure, he warned us. But I'm not convinced that he meant *he* was going to chase us away. Unless . . ."

"What?" Joe demanded.

"Wait a minute," Frank said. His thoughts were swirling around in his head. "Listen, we've taken for granted what Mike told us, that his business is going to be ruined if people start thinking the tours are jinxed. But how do we know that's so? He's got a full group this time, doesn't he? And that's *after* that story in the tabloid about the girl who got hurt."

"Jessica signed up, and she actually knows the girl in the newspaper story," Joe said.

Frank nodded. "Good point. The chances are, more people heard about Teen Trails West from reading that story than any other way. And a few months from now, chances are they'll still remember the name, but not the jinx."

"Are you saying that Mike has been sabotaging his own operation, for the publicity?"

"I find it hard to believe," Frank replied, shrugging. "But I *am* saying we have to keep the possibility in mind. Alex still tops the list of suspects, in my opinion, but we'd better keep an eye on everyone . . . *everyone*."

The Hardys rejoined the group around the campfire. The teens seemed to have recovered from the sniper incident somewhat, thanks to Greg's accordion playing.

After a few more songs, Tom told a Hopi folktale about a boy who was kidnapped by eagles and who passed through many trials and acquired much wisdom before he was allowed to return to his people.

"Our trials together, the last two days, are much smaller than his were," Tom concluded, looking gravely around the circle of faces. "But maybe we, too, will be granted some wisdom before we return to our homes and families."

Subdued but calm, the members of the group found their tents and went to sleep. Frank stayed up. He and Joe had decided to divide the night into two watches, and he had taken the first.

During his watch, Frank walked slowly around the campsite to keep from falling asleep. The only disturbance the entire time was a low-flying owl. Finally Frank returned to the tent he was sharing with Joe. It was the last in the row and nearest the chuck wagon, which loomed up strangely in the darkness. He woke Joe and crawled into his sleeping bag.

Later that night, Frank dreamed that he was

camped on the banks of a rushing mountain stream. The sound wasn't soothing. He didn't dare to move a muscle in his dream. If he were to slip off the bank, still in his sleeping bag, he would surely drown before he disentangled himself.

Frank woke up at first light to a very different sound. Nearby, an angry Billy Bob was muttering loudly.

"That stinking sidewinder! If I catch up with the buzzard who did this, I swear I'll skin him alive!"

Frank looked over at Joe's sleeping bag. It was empty. As he reached for his jeans, he heard Billy Bob call, "Mike, you better get over here. We've got us a big problem."

Frank stumbled out of the tent and saw Mike running toward the chuck wagon, where a grim-faced Billy Bob was waiting. Joe was by his side. Frank ran in that direction. As he rounded the corner of the chuck wagon, Frank's foot slipped on a very wet patch of mud. In a corner of his mind, he noted how odd that was—it hadn't rained during the night.

Billy Bob, Joe, and Mike were staring at the rack on the side of the chuck wagon. It held the three large jerricans that contained the drinking water for the tour. Frank looked closer, and then his eyebrows shot up in surprise. Two of the jerricans were empty. There was a neat round hole punched in each of their sides. Below the holes, the wooden rack was still damp.

"Well, now," Mike said in a soft voice. He seemed

calm, but Frank noticed that his fists were so tightly clenched that the knuckles were white.

Billy Bob lifted one of the punctured jerricans out of the rack and silently shook it.

"Well, now," Mike repeated. "I reckon we just found out what that varmint last night was shooting at!"

11 A Saboteur
Is Exposed

"So that's the situation," Mike said. He had just told the members of the group about the punctured water cans. "Sometime tomorrow, we'll reach a spring with good water. We can stock up again once we're there. In the meantime, I'm counting on all of you to save water any way you can think of."

Joe scanned the group. Almost everyone was taking Mike's news very seriously. The exception was Jessica, who seemed to think this was one more stunt that had been planned to make the trip more interesting.

Nick raised his hand. "What about the horses? We're not going to let them go thirsty, are we?"

"Better them than us," Jessica said.

Alex said, "That's just the kind of attitude I'd expect from you."

As Jessica opened her mouth to retort, Mike jumped in. "Hold it! No bickering, and no personal remarks. Is that clear? We're going to have to pull together, all of us. Maybe we're facing one of those trials that Tom was talking about in his story last night. And to answer Nick's question, no, we won't let the horses go thirsty. A few miles from here, the trail starts following a stream that they can drink from. It might upset our tummies, but not theirs. They're not as picky about their drinking water as we are.

"Now," he added, "let's see about some breakfast. We'll skip the tea and coffee, but we still have orange juice."

While people started lining up for breakfast, Mike took Joe and Frank aside.

"I wasn't being completely honest just now," he admitted. "The situation's worse than I made it sound."

"How much worse?" Joe asked.

"Well . . . by the time we get to that spring I told them about, we're all going to be thinking we've got our mouths packed with cotton balls. And that's if everything goes the way I hope it will."

"And if anything else goes wrong?" Frank probed.

"Then we're in real trouble," Mike replied. "With most of the water gone, we've got no room for mistakes, and that's not any way I want to operate when I'm in charge of other people's kids."

He took a deep breath and added, "The fact is, I'm just about a hair away from calling it quits. I can crank up the CB right now and ask one of the hands back at the ranch to bring out more water, but if I do, everybody in the country is going to know about it. Once that happens, I'm finished. But you know what? I'm starting to think that might be a relief!"

Joe exchanged glances with Frank. It was pretty clear to both of them that Mike was *not* sabotaging his operation for the publicity. He seemed much too upset.

Finally Joe said, "Mike? Will you hold off, just for twenty-four hours? If we can show that someone's been trying to sabotage you, and prove who it is, Teen Trails will be safe."

Mike knitted his brows. "Do you think you know the guy in back of this?" he demanded. "Who is it?"

"We don't have the evidence to start naming names," Joe replied. "But how about it? Can we have until breakfast-time tomorrow?"

Mike took off his hat and stared down into it, as if he expected to find the answer there. Finally he said, "I asked you two out here to do a job. It's only fair that I give you a chance to do it."

"Great," Joe said. "We'll do our best. Now, I'd love to have a big glass of that orange juice!"

Mike laughed and threw a punch at his arm. Then, with a wave that was part salute, he went back to the group.

"Do you mind waiting a few minutes until breakfast?" Frank asked Joe. "I'd like to look over that hilltop by daylight."

"Good idea," Joe replied. "Let's go."

At the crest of the hill, Frank turned for a look at

the camp. He could make out the faces of all the people eating breakfast. The chuck wagon, on the near side of the camp, seemed close enough to reach out and touch. The sniper didn't have to be an expert marksman to have hit the jerricans. It was a wonder he hadn't holed all three of them.

The hiding place between the two boulders looked much as it had the night before. The soft ground had been scuffed by so many boots that finding any of the rifleman's prints was a hopeless task.

Joe was sitting on his haunches, studying the ground from close up. Suddenly his hand darted forward and picked up something.

"What did you find?" Frank asked.

"A burnt paper match," Joe said. His voice was heavy with disappointment. "So now we know the sniper smokes and won't spend a buck for a lighter. Terrific."

Frank looked at the match. "Burnt to past halfway," he pointed out. "Our friend with the rifle must have had trouble lighting his cigarette. There wasn't much wind last night, was there?"

Joe considered it, then shook his head.

"Hmm . . ." Frank continued. "He didn't seem to be worried about anybody seeing the match flame or smelling the cigarette smoke, did he? Funny way for a sniper to act. Do you recall if Crazy Jake smoked?"

Joe shrugged. "No idea. Anyway, maybe our guy only smoked while we were all away on that hike," he suggested.

"We weren't *all* away," Frank replied. "Remember,

Billy Bob was right down there, just a stone's throw away, working on the chuck wagon."

"Well, maybe he was *under* the chuck wagon and couldn't see. Or maybe he's the sniper. I don't know! No, that doesn't work. He was down with the rest of us when we heard the shots. Come on, let's see what else we can learn, then go back. I'm so hungry that even the idea of canned orange juice makes my mouth water!"

The Hardys went around to the back of the two boulders and began to study the ground, making wide sweeps that took them farther and farther from the sniper's nest.

"I don't get it," Joe said when they met up at the end of a sweep. "There are plenty of soft spots, but not a print anywhere. No boot prints, hoofprints, tire prints . . . Did the sniper have wings?"

"It's beginning to look that way," Frank replied. "Here, let's go over what we know."

He counted on his outstretched fingers. "One, he hid between those rocks. Two, while we were all gathered around the fire, he let off three shots. Three, his bullets hit the water cans. And four, he somehow managed to get clean out of sight in the time it took Billy Bob to run up the hill. We have solid physical evidence for numbers one through three, and nothing at all to show how he pulled off his escape. It's not as if he had time to erase his tracks with a broom!"

Suddenly Frank stiffened. "Joe," he said softly. "Don't turn around, don't make a sign. There's someone spying on us from behind a big bush, about twenty feet behind you, a little to your left. We'll rush him on three. You go left, I'll go right. One . . . two . . ."

As "Three!" left his lips, Frank sprinted toward the bush, shoulder to shoulder with his brother. Just as the Hardys rounded the bush from opposite directions, a ragged figure backed away, his palms toward them in a pleading gesture. Frank recognized the battered hat even before he saw the long white beard and piercing blue eyes. It was Crazy Jake.

"You wouldn't hurt old Jake, who never did you any harm?" the prospector said in a trembling voice.

"What about shooting holes in our water cans?" Joe demanded. "You don't call that harm?"

"I never!" the old man insisted, standing straighter. Indignation replaced the fear in his voice.

"Where's your rifle, Jake?" Frank asked. "The barrel will show if it was fired last night."

Jake gave him a sly, sidelong look. "It's put away, someplace safe," he said. "Someplace *they'll* never find it. Or you either."

"Who are 'they,' Jake?" Joe asked roughly. "The law?"

Confusion replaced slyness in the old man's eyes. "I don't know," he mumbled. "They want to scare me away, so they can steal my . . . my property."

Frank remembered Mike's account of Jake and knew that the words he had bit back were "uranium mine."

"Mike has never hurt me or made fun of me," the grizzled prospector continued. "He'll let me come along. He'll protect me from them."

107

Frank met Joe's eyes and shrugged. Was the old man for real? And even if he was, he was not the usual Teen Trails West participant.

"Er . . . we can ask Mike," Frank began. "But we're on horseback, you know. How would you keep up?"

Jake stared at him, then stuck two fingers in his mouth and let out a shrill whistle. Moments later, a swaybacked white and gray horse ambled into view. It stopped just behind the old man and dropped its head to graze. Jake turned to stroke its mane.

Frank asked, "Jake? Do you know a guy named Roy Ramirez? Is he one of the people you're talking about?"

Jake pretended to be totally wrapped up in stroking his horse.

"How do we know you're not working for Ramirez?" Joe added. "Mike won't take you along if you're on the side of his enemies."

"There's enemies and enemies," Jake replied. "There's folks you plain don't like, and there's folks who'll do you dirty every chance they get."

"Which kind is Ramirez?" Frank pursued.

Jake shrugged. "I don't know. But I'm not Mike's enemy. He knows that."

"There's another problem," Joe said. "We're short on water. Like we said, somebody shot holes in our water cans last night."

The sly look was back on the old man's face. "They do dirty tricks like that. But I know tricks they don't. I know springs that no one else knows, not even that

108

Indian who rides with you. If Mike lets me come along, he won't have to worry about water."

Frank exchanged another look with Joe, then said, "You'd better come and talk to Mike yourself."

The old man led his horse on his own route down the hill, one that got him there right after Frank and Joe. The camp was already struck, and most of the riders had finished saddling and bridling their mounts.

"You better hurry, you guys," Mike said, then looked curiously at their companion and added, "Morning, Jake. How are you doing? What brings you to these parts?"

Jake looked at Frank and said, "You tell him."

Joe wandered off to pack up their gear, and Frank began to explain as best he could. He was just beginning to tell Mike about Jake's offer to find water for them when he was interrupted by a loud commotion. Most of the campers were standing in a circle. Joe was at the center of it.

Joe was standing right in front of Jessica, just inches away from her. She kept trying to dodge past him, and he kept stepping into her path.

"Get out of my way, you hoodlum!" she shouted. "I'm going to sue you for everything you've got."

"Not a chance, Jessica," Joe replied, just as loudly. "Don't try to wriggle out of it. You're the one who's been trying to wreck this tour, but this time I caught you in the act!"

12 The Anasazi Connection

Jessica landed a kick on Joe's left shin and tried to run past him on the left. He stretched out his arms and blocked her again. She looked around and saw the others, standing shoulder to shoulder. Her face reddened, and she made a dash headlong into Mike, who caught her before she fell.

"What's all this about?" Mike demanded.

Joe stepped forward and said, "Just now, I noticed Jessica pick something up off the ground and slip it under her horse's saddle blanket."

Mike turned. "Is this true, Jessica?"

Jessica raised her chin and looked right past him.

Mike turned to the horse and slipped his hand under the rear of the blanket. Then he pulled his hand out and held up a sharp-edged piece of flint.

"Do you know that this would have cut into Cinnamon's back when you got into the saddle?" he demanded angrily.

Jessica stayed silent, but a troubled expression crossed her face.

"If there's one thing I hate," Mike continued, "it's cruelty to animals. Especially deliberate cruelty. And I can't say I much care for dishonesty and treachery, either. I'm going to radio the ranch and tell Charlie to come out and get you. He'll call your parents and put you on a plane home."

"No, please!" Jessica cried. "I didn't mean to hurt Cinnamon. She's the only one who's treated me like a friend."

"But you admit you put that rock under the blanket," Joe said.

She refused to look in his direction. "Yeah," she muttered.

"So she'd buck when you got on," Frank probed.

"Yeah. I was planning to fall off right away, though. Neither one of us would have gotten hurt."

"You loosened the cinch strap yourself, didn't you?" Mike said, grim-faced. "And pulled that stunt with the stirrup strap. And you tried to throw the blame on Alex and Nick, knowing they were innocent."

"Yes, yes, yes!" Jessica cried. "I had to do something! I didn't want to come on this crummy trip in the first place. It was all my mom's idea. But then when nerdy Lorna Bradley got her picture on the front page of that tabloid and started telling everybody at our school how famous she was, I figured maybe I could get something good out of the trip after all. If she could get so much attention with such a dumb publicity stunt, so could I."

Frank frowned. "Publicity stunt? Are you saying that Lorna caused her own accident?"

"Of course she did," Jessica replied. "She even bragged about it to me. But she made sure to do it when no one else was around. Those bandages wrapped around her wrist were just for sympathy. There was nothing wrong with her wrist—she even beat me in tennis."

Joe figured it was time to join the questioning. "I can see how these accidents of yours might be good for some publicity, especially after what happened to your friend Lorna," he said. "But what about the chuck wagon's brakes? Nick and I were almost killed."

"I didn't do anything to the brakes on the chuck wagon," Jessica said, almost shouting. "How could I? I don't even know how they work!"

"And the pins in the saddle blankets?" Frank asked. "What about that?"

Jessica looked frantically from person to person, as if hoping to find a sympathetic face. "I already *told* you! I loosened my cinch strap and shortened my stirrup, and I put that rock under my saddle just now, but that's *it*! And I wouldn't have loosened the cinch strap if I'd known I'd nearly be dragged to death. You can believe me or not, but it's the truth!" She burst into tears.

Carina came over, put her arm around Jessica's shoulders, and turned her away from the crowd. "There's no need to badger her," Carina said, and led the sobbing Jessica away.

Shaking his head, Mike followed the two girls.

"Well?" Joe said to Frank. "What do you think?"

"I think you just solved part of the mystery," Frank replied. "Good work."

Joe scowled with frustration. "Not good enough, though. I believed her about the brakes on the chuck wagon. Whoever weakened the cable knew just what he—or she—was doing. Jessica's the kind who takes her car to the mechanic if the ashtray's full."

Frank said, "You're probably right, unless she's putting one over on us."

"And there's the little matter of the sniper," Joe continued grimly. "All in all, this case is far from being closed."

Mike came over to them just then, looking sheepish. "I think maybe we were a little too rough on Jessica. She just talked me into letting her finish the tour." He glanced at his wristwatch and added, "We'd better hit the trail. We'll have to take a long break during the heat of the day. The horses will need it, even if we don't."

Just before noon, the caravan halted in a small grove of juniper trees. Tom took the horses down to the stream to drink, while Billy Bob started a fire and began preparing what he announced would be a very special stew.

"Oof!" Joe groaned, dropping his hat on the grass and lying down full-length in the shade. "It's like an oven out here!"

Frank sat down beside him and mopped his forehead. "I saw some dark clouds to the west," he replied. "Maybe we'll have a shower to cool things off."

"Yeah, sure," Joe said. "And maybe we'll find one of those springs that Jake told us about. I'll settle for the one that gives ice-cold lemonade."

Overhead, the branches of the trees swayed wildly as a sudden cool breeze hit them. Moments later, the sky darkened. Not long after, a brilliant flash of blue light was followed by a crash of thunder that echoed from every direction. Raindrops that felt as big as marbles made miniature craters in the dust.

Everyone crowded under the trees with Frank and Joe. The shoulders of Mike's work shirt were soaked, but he had a grin on his face.

"Anybody know 'The Old Chisholm Trail'?" Mike asked. "I just thought of my favorite verse." He sang, "'Clouds in the west, it looks like rain, and my danged old slicker's in the wagon again!'"

Jessica, huddling under a rain-soaked scarf, looked at them as if she were sure they had just lost their minds. But when Mike launched into another verse of the old cowpuncher's song, Joe noticed that Jessica joined the rest of the group on the chorus. Even Jake sang along, in a voice that sounded like a rusty gate hinge.

"Shouldn't we put out buckets or something?" Carina asked.

"Not much point," Mike replied. "These cloud-bursts generally end as quick as they begin."

As if on cue, the shower ended. Billy Bob returned to his cook fire, while the others chatted, wrote postcards, and read.

"Carina," Tom said, "I haven't forgotten my promise to show you an Anasazi site. There is a village near here that has never been excavated. We could walk there in fifteen minutes, if you like."

"Can I come, too?" Lisa asked.

"Me, too," Alex said, jumping to his feet. "Hey, Lisa, you can get some great pictures."

"Do you mind if I come along?" Joe asked, after exchanging a quick look with Frank. They didn't want to let Alex out of their sight.

"Okay," Tom said, "but that's enough for one trip. These ruins are fragile. We don't want to damage them. If anybody feels left out, I'll take another group to look at a different site when we stop for the day."

Frank gave Joe a nod and went off to talk to Mike.

From their stopping place by the creek, Tom led the little group up along a gulch with walls twenty feet high. A tiny stream, just inches wide, trickled along the bottom of the gully. But when Joe glanced upward, he noticed tree branches wedged among the rocks fifteen feet up, carried there by the raging waters of flash floods.

Soon they came to a spot where the walls of the

gully changed from straight up and down to a slope of about forty-five degrees.

"We go this way," Tom said. "I'll get halfway up and give you each a hand."

Joe went last. He found footholds among the jumbled rocks, but he was glad for the help from Tom. When Joe reached the rim, he saw that they were standing on a mesa top, dotted with tall, bayonet-leaved yucca plants. Perhaps encouraged by the recent shower, some of them displayed central spikes of cream-colored flowers.

"The Anasazi could live in such barren country because they were wise in its ways," Tom told them. "Take the yucca—they made rope from the fiber in its leaves, ground the pods into flour, and even used the roots for their soap and shampoo."

Lisa went over to one of the yuccas and took a close-up of the flowers.

The group walked across the mesa toward a depression in the ground. Going closer, Joe could see what looked like waist-high walls and began to experience an excitement he hadn't expected to feel about thousand-year-old ruins.

From the edge of the hollow it was clear that the stone walls had once formed houses with many rooms.

"Can we go down and look around?" Carina asked eagerly.

"Yes, if you are careful. There is a path there, to your left," Tom said.

Carina led the way, followed by Alex and Lisa. Joe brought up the rear. As they reached the level of the ruins, he noticed that some of the piled-up earth was a different color and seemed less packed down.

"Tom?" Joe called. "Could you come down here? There's something I want you to see."

Tom joined him, and Joe pointed to the place he had noticed, where the earth was a darker shade of brown. Tom became very still. Then he kneeled down and peered at the ground. When he stood up, his face was dark with anger. He called the others back.

"People have been digging here," he reported. "They tried to hide what they have done, but it is obvious if you know where to look."

"Pothunters?" Carina asked.

Tom shook his head. "No. Pothunters usually scratch the surface. They do not dig deep, in search of grave sites. The color of the upturned earth tells me that these are professional looters. They have done terrible damage to this site, and very recently—in the last day or two." He turned to Lisa. "I want you to take pictures—*lots* of pictures."

Lisa gulped and said, "Sure, Tom."

"Come," Tom said. "You others, stay here. If you wander, you may erase important signs without knowing it."

Joe waited with Carina and Alex. Could this damage have been done by the people whom Jake called "them"? Joe longed to start scouring the site, looking for clues, instead of standing still playing spectator. But he couldn't, not without blowing his cover and alerting one of his chief suspects—Alex.

Tom returned, deeply angry. "This is the fourth

117

pillaged Anasazi site I have seen this summer, just among those I have happened to visit," he said. "Greedy men are stealing the heritage of the Native Americans. They must be stopped!"

"Tom?" Joe said. "It isn't easy to get to this site. I bet the looters used a jeep. I spotted one earlier. It must have left tracks. I know you looked all around inside the ruins, but what about farther away?"

Tom looked embarrassed. "You are right. I was too mad to think clearly," he said. "Come. We will make a big circle, looking for the marks of their tires."

Two-thirds of the way around the site, Alex shouted, "There! I see something!" He started to rush forward, but Joe was ready for just such a move. He grabbed Alex's arm and held him back. He didn't want him to erase any evidence.

"Let Tom look them over first," Joe said.

"Sure," Alex replied, giving him a look of irritation and puzzlement.

Tom went forward, then beckoned to Lisa, who took a half dozen pictures of the tire tracks. As she finished, Joe moved forward and took a close look at the tracks. The superwide off-road tires had a distinctive tread pattern that he had never seen before.

"Thanks, Joe," Tom said. "We had better get back to camp. They'll be starting to worry about us."

"Worse than that," Carina said. "They'll be starting lunch without us!"

* * *

The moment they got back, Joe took Frank aside and filled him in on what the little expedition had found.

"I'm ready to bet that the tracks will match up with those from the jeep I spotted earlier," Joe concluded.

"Ramirez?" Frank asked. "If so, that might mean that he and his bunch are really grave robbers, and Alex's job is to see to it that Mike and his groups stay away from the digs."

Joe nodded. "This is beginning to hang together. Robbing Indian relics is a very big, very profitable business."

"*And* very illegal," Frank pointed out.

"Right. So when Mike started bringing his Teen Trails tours through here, it threatened to expose the operation. Result? The crooks decided to put him out of business for good."

Frank was opening his mouth to add to this explanation when Billy Bob started banging the triangle for lunch. Frank and Joe joined the line, accepted plates of steaming stew thick with carrots, potatoes, and onions, and carried them over to where Carina, Greg, and Mike were sitting.

Greg dug his fork into his stew and took a bite. Suddenly he sprang up, overturning his plate on the ground. Red-faced, he clapped his hands over his mouth.

"Water!" he gasped. *"Water!"*

119

13 Missing Evidence

All around the campsite, people were fanning their open mouths while tears rolled down their cheeks. Billy Bob looked at them in bewilderment, then dipped a spoon into the big stew pot.

"Whoo-ee!" he shouted, after tasting a small bite. "How'd it get to have such an almighty kick?"

"We'll figure that out later," Mike said grimly, pouring out cups of water from the last of their precious supply. Carina, who hadn't tried the stew yet, helped take them around to those who were obviously suffering the worst.

Frank hadn't tasted the stew yet, either. He took a piece of carrot on his fork and cautiously touched it with the tip of his tongue. He immediately felt a four-alarm blaze. He shuddered to think what a whole forkful would have done to his mouth.

"The saboteur strikes again," Joe murmured, just loud enough for Frank to hear. "Either that, or Billy Bob is the most careless cook on this side of the Continental Divide."

"Our saboteur plans well," Frank added. "First the water supply, then this."

Billy Bob was rummaging around in the back of the chuck wagon. Suddenly he turned around and loudly demanded, "Who's the funny guy who did this? Come on, admit it!"

The auburn-haired cook waved a small glass jar over his head. Frank went closer and looked at it. The label said Chopped Jalapeños. The jar was empty.

"Someone put a whole jar of Mexican hot peppers in the stew?" Frank asked.

Billy Bob nodded grimly. "I just opened it the other night, and I didn't use but one teaspoonful. That was good stew I just made, before some joker messed with it."

"*When* did he mess with it?" Joe asked. "When did you taste it last?"

Billy Bob looked away. "Well," he said, "the fact is, once it was going good, I didn't taste it again. I didn't figure I needed to. That was about an hour ago."

"Did you stay near it while it cooked? Who had a chance to put something in it?" Frank asked.

"Say, you boys are regular detectives, aren't you?" he replied. "Lemme see—yeah, I was nearby the whole time, except a couple of times when I had to do some prep on the rest of lunch. But that's okay. I had Alex watch the stew and give it a stir from time to time. Then he went off with Tom and the others, so I passed his job on to Nick."

Frank gave Joe a look full of meaning. Alex again! He had the opportunity to doctor the stew, and, if their theory was right, a motive as well. And the means—the jar of hot peppers—had been sitting in the chuck wagon, waiting for him to take them. Of course, Billy Bob had means and opportunity, too, but what would his motive be?

"I think it's time we had a talk with Alex," Joe said.

"I agree," Frank replied. "Mike had better be in on this. I'll go get him."

Alex was a little apart from the others, leaning against a tree, jotting in a notebook. He glanced up as Frank, Joe, and Mike approached. Frank saw a flash of alarm in his face.

"Alex?" Mike began. "I think you'd better level with me about your being hitched up with Roy Ramirez."

Alex sighed. "I *knew* I couldn't keep it a secret. I'm such a blabbermouth, things just kept slipping out that gave me away. Who figured it out?"

"We did," Frank said. He didn't want to admit that he had searched Alex's pack. "How do you know Ramirez?"

Alex gave him a puzzled glance. "I thought you'd figured that out, too. I went on an ORA expedition last

122

summer. It was great, but while I was out there, I heard about Teen Trails West and decided I'd like to see this country again, but from horseback. When I told Roy, he took it pretty hard. He thought I'd be going with him again this year. But he got over it. Then he told me that he and Mike weren't getting along very well. He said it might be better if I didn't tell anybody about my ORA trip."

He paused and looked at Frank, Mike, and Joe, then added, "I can see by the way you're looking at me that he was right, too." He sounded bitter.

"What did Ramirez tell you to do while you were on this tour?" Joe demanded, a little roughly.

"Huh? What do you mean?" Alex asked, his blue eyes growing large.

"A lot of things have been happening on the tour," Frank said. "Some might be practical jokes, like the hot peppers in the stew just now, but there was nothing funny about sabotaging the brakes on the chuck wagon."

"Now, wait a minute—" Alex began.

"Listen, Alex," Mike said in a soft voice. "I've got to find out who's responsible and stop him or her, before somebody gets badly hurt. You can understand that."

"Why are you talking to me?" Alex demanded.

"You were seen under the chuck wagon before the brakes failed," Joe told him. "And you had the best chance to doctor the stew today. If anyone wanted to ruin Mike's business—a competitor, let's say— having an accomplice on the inside working for him would be a pretty shrewd move, wouldn't it? As long as the connection between the competitor and the person on the inside stayed a secret."

Alex stood taller and brushed his sandy hair away from his forehead. "Just hold it right there," he said. "If you're saying that I've been pulling those tricks, because Roy asked me to, you are way off base. If you don't believe me, ask him."

"If he's trying to ruin Mike, he's not going to admit it—especially if he's the sniper who went after our water supply," Joe said. "You'll have to do better than that, Alex."

"How do you expect me to prove I *didn't* do something?" Alex demanded. "What am I supposed to have done, anyway?"

"What were you doing under the chuck wagon yesterday during the lunch break?" Frank asked.

"How should I know? I don't even remember being under the chuck wagon."

"You were," Joe said. "You threw your Frisbee under it and went after it. Twice."

Alex shrugged. "Then that's your answer. I was getting my Frisbee."

"And cutting the brake cable at the same time," Joe added.

"I'd *never* do a thing like that," Alex insisted. "Somebody could get hurt. But if I did, you can bet I'd make sure nobody saw me do it.

"Look," he continued, turning to Mike. "I don't have to put up with this. I paid a lot of money to come on this trip, and I have a right to be treated the same as everyone else. Why don't you try your third degree on Jessica? She already admitted pulling a bunch of dirty tricks. Is it because her dad's an important Hollywood director, and mine's a dentist in St. Louis? Let me tell you something, Mike. That stinks!" He pushed between Frank and Joe and stalked away.

Mike watched him go, then said, "He's got a point. It's not fair to ask him to prove he's innocent. We don't have any proof he's guilty."

"Not yet, we don't," Joe said. "He can say anything he likes, but he's still our best suspect. And if we keep a close enough watch on him, we'll get the proof we need."

"If I felt sure of that," Mike said, "I'd send him home right away and refund his money. And the same with Jessica. I don't want to throw anybody in jail. I just want to keep my tours going."

Frank said, "I agree we should keep an eye on Alex, but I can't help feeling that we're missing something important."

"Hey, guys," Lisa called. "Get over here. I want to get some shots of the whole group."

Frank looked around. Everyone else was standing in front of the chuck wagon, looking self-conscious. Lisa, facing them, was checking the controls of her camera, which was mounted on a tripod.

Mike and the Hardys joined the group, just as Lisa said, "I'm using the self-timer, so I can be in the picture, too. When I push the button, it'll start beeping. When the beeps stop, it takes the pictures. I set it to take two in a row, so don't move after the first one. Everybody ready?"

She pressed the shutter release, then walked quickly over to join the group. As the beeps began, Frank found himself staring at the lens of the camera with a fixed smile on his face. He risked a quick glance around and saw that the others were doing the same—all but Joe, who was holding his fingers in a V behind Mike's head. Joe caught Frank's glance and pulled his hand down.

The beeps stopped, but instead of the click of the shutter and the whir of the film winder, there was a longer, deeper beep.

"Oops! Sorry, people," Lisa said. "That means something's wrong. Just a sec."

She hurried over and examined the controls, then straightened up with a baffled look on her face. "The film's gone," she announced. "Somebody took the film out of my camera!"

"Are you sure it was loaded?" Carina asked.

"Of course I am!"

Frank stepped forward. "When was the last time you checked your camera, Lisa?"

"Why—when we were coming back from our walk. Then Alex offered to carry it for me, so I gave it to him."

Frank turned and caught Joe's eye, then looked at Alex.

"Oh, no, you don't," Alex exclaimed. "All I did was

carry the camera back to camp. Then I gave it to Nick to put with Lisa's stuff. I never took any film out of it."

Joe went over to Frank and said softly, "That roll of film must be important. But Alex was the one who urged Lisa to take pictures on our hike. Why would he do that, then steal the film?"

"I don't know," Frank replied. Aloud he said, "Nick, do you know anything about the missing film?"

Nick, wide-eyed, said, "Me? Not a thing. I put the camera in Lisa's gadget bag, right before lunch."

Billy Bob broke in. "If we're not going to have our picture taken, I'm going to get ready to hit the trail. Okay?"

His colorfully decorated cowboy boots were under the chuck wagon, in the shade. He pulled them out and slipped off one of the moccasins he always wore around camp.

"In these parts, it's usually a good idea to shake out your boots before you put them on," he said, turning the boot upside down. "You can never tell what—"

Greg gasped. Jessica bit her knuckle to hold back a scream.

A two-inch-long centipede fell out of Billy Bob's boot and landed in the dirt. Its dozens of legs carried it scurrying toward the group, with its poison-filled fangs ready to strike.

14 Stampede!

Mike took two quick steps forward and brought the high heel of his western boot down on the head of the centipede. Then he turned to Nick and said, in a mild voice, "Weren't you telling me, just this morning, that you'd caught yourself a centipede?"

Nick blinked a couple of times. "Why . . . yes, I did."

"Where is it now?"

"With my stuff, I guess," Nick replied. "But don't worry, it's safe. I put it in a plastic box that's specially made for collecting insects."

Joe looked over the area under the chuck wagon where Billy Bob's boots had been standing. After a minute of searching the rocky ground he straightened up and said, "Something like this?"

128

Everyone turned to look at the clear plastic box with air holes that Joe was holding.

"That's it," Nick said in a puzzled voice. "But . . . where's my centipede?"

Joe pointed at the ground. "Under Mike's heel," he said. "And before that, it was in Billy Bob's boot. Now, don't tell me that it lifted the lid of this box, got out, and crawled into that boot, taking special care to put the lid back on the box first."

"Don't be silly," Nick replied. "Obviously somebody took it and put it in the boot."

Suddenly Nick understood what Joe was hinting at. "You think *I* put the centipede there? That's crazy! Why would I do a thing like that? Do you have any idea how hard I had to work to catch one in the first place? And now it's squashed."

Joe studied Nick's face. He seemed sincerely distressed and angry about the loss of the centipede.

Frank stepped in and asked, "Who knew you'd caught the centipede?"

Nick shrugged. "I don't know . . . I told Mike and Billy Bob about it. And I showed it to Alex when I was putting it away in my pack. That's it, I guess."

"*I* didn't know, that's for sure," Jessica insisted, hands on her hips. "I'd have made you get rid of that creepy thing!" She gave an exaggerated shudder.

"People like you have really messed-up attitudes about insects," Nick said. "If you just took the trouble to understand . . ."

Joe took Frank's arm and led him away from the

group, near where the horses were tethered. "Well?" he said. "Any ideas?"

Frank frowned. "I think we can cross Jessica off, for this one anyway. She'd rather be caught wearing last year's hot brand of designer jeans than go anywhere near a centipede."

Joe smirked. "I'm with you there. And Nick's just the opposite—he liked that ugly bug too much to use it for a prank. Not that we have even a glimmer of a motive for him, anyway. So we come back to Alex. Same motive as before, and he's got means and opportunity as well."

"And we've still got zip in the way of evidence against him," Frank replied, leaning against a tree. "All we can say is that he *could* have pulled off most of the dirty tricks, and the ones he couldn't, like the sniper attack on the water cans, could have been the work of Roy Ramirez. Or even Jake. But wait . . . Who took Lisa's film, and why?"

Joe thought for a few moments. "Maybe she accidentally took a picture of someone—Alex, let's say—in the act of carrying out a dirty trick. That'd be good, solid evidence."

"Another big *maybe*," Frank retorted, kicking a rock in frustration. "What do we know for sure? Lisa took pictures of an Anasazi village that had been pillaged, and of what are probably the tire tracks of the skunks who did it. Talk about solid evidence! And when she got back to camp, somebody stole the film. A coincidence? It could be, but I doubt it."

"The grave robbers!" Joe suddenly exclaimed.

"They don't want Mike's tours coming through here, because it gets in the way of their operation, so they're using the dirty tricks to destroy Teen Tours. And somebody in our group could be working with the grave robbers!"

"But wait a minute," Joe added, after thinking his hunch through. "What if Ramirez's operation is really a front for grave robbing? He'd have the best of excuses to be driving around the back country. Then Mike came along and cramped his style. In that case, Alex could still be his inside man."

"That's possible," Frank said. "On the other hand—" He broke off what he was saying as Lisa came walking over to them.

"Joe," she said in a troubled voice, "I didn't tell the whole truth just now."

"What do you mean?"

"About the missing film. I . . . Do you remember when I took all those pictures of the digging at the village, and the tire tracks and all?"

"Sure. Well?"

She nibbled at the inside of her cheek for a moment, then said, "I took so many shots that I had to put in a fresh roll of film. Whoever took the film out of my camera got the new roll—there were no pictures on it yet."

"Where's the other one?" Frank demanded. "Is it safe?"

She gave him a sidelong glance, then looked back at Joe. "I want you to keep this for me," she said. She slipped a black plastic film container into his hand.

131

"I'm scared. If the people who took the other one find out they made a mistake, they might come looking for it."

"Don't worry, Lisa," Joe said. "We'll look after it for you."

"Somehow I knew I could count on you," she said. Glancing at Frank, she added, "Both of you."

As she walked away, Frank said, "That's a big promise you just made."

Joe gave him a challenging glance. "I'm big enough to carry it out," he said. Then he grinned and said, "With a little family cooperation, of course!"

There were no further incidents during the afternoon, but by dinnertime, everyone was on edge. Little arguments broke out, not just between Alex and Jessica, as usual, but between Nick and Lisa and between Tom and Billy Bob. Even the twins, Greg and Carina, were short-tempered with each other.

At bedtime, Frank took Joe aside and said, "I'm worried about tonight. I think we ought to keep a watch."

"I was going to say the same thing," Joe replied. "Two-hour shifts sound okay? I'll volunteer for ten to twelve and two to four."

By five-thirty in the morning, Frank was starting to think that the watches were wasted effort. Nothing at all had disturbed the camp during the night. He was sitting on an elevated rocky outcrop that gave him a panoramic view of the horses, tents, and chuck wagon. The sky in the east was turning a lighter shade, and the brilliant field of stars was fading. The mesas in the distance were silhouetted by the rosy light, and Frank heard the faraway cry of a lone hawk. Before long, it would be wake-up time.

Frank was wondering if he would be able to find a few moments during the day for a nap when he heard one of the horses whinny. A moment later, another snorted loudly. Something was disturbing the herd. As quietly as he could, Frank walked over to check it out.

As he was passing a big cottonwood tree, he heard a faint sound behind him. He started to turn, but at that moment something hit him, hard, just behind the ear. He fell to his hands and knees, stunned by the blow, but he managed to hang on to a few shreds of consciousness, enough to notice that his attacker was wearing fancy boots.

He was starting to push himself upright, with a little help from the tree trunk, when he heard someone shout, "Hey-yah!" A moment later, dozens of hooves started to pound the earth.

Frank looked around. In the predawn light, he saw the herd of horses mill around, then break into a panic-stricken run. Horrified, he realized that the stampeding herd was headed straight toward him. It was too late to run. In moments he would be trampled under their steel-shod hooves!

15 Into the Sunset

Frank pulled himself to his feet. The stampeding horses were almost upon him. He looked around frantically for any means of escape.

Overhead, just out of reach, was a branch that looked thick enough to hold his weight. Grimly determined, he crouched down and sprang. His right hand grasped the branch, but his left hand missed. He took a deep breath and did a one-armed chin-up, grabbing with his other hand as soon as it could reach the branch. A second later, he pulled himself up onto the branch, just as the horses thundered past the spot where he had been standing.

Star, Frank's black mount, was near the back of the herd. Frank noticed that the horse seemed less panicked than the others, who were moving at a frenzy right underneath him. As Star passed under Frank's branch, he let himself drop onto the horse's back. Taken by surprise, Star reared back and almost scraped Frank off against the tree that had been his refuge. Then, as Frank wrapped his arms around the horse's neck, Star took off at a gallop after the rest of the herd.

"Whoa, Star, you remember me," Frank said. "I'm the one who feeds you carrots and gives you long drinks." Star seemed to recognize Frank's voice. As the horse calmed down, Frank used the touch of his hands on the sides of Star's neck to guide him back to the campsite. But as he slid off Star's back, someone suddenly yanked him by the shoulder, spun him around, and grabbed a handful of his shirtfront.

It was Tom. His face was distorted with rage, and his huge fist was drawn back to give Frank a knockout punch.

He shouted, "You ran off my horses, you—"

The last word was in a language Frank didn't recognize, but he could tell that it wasn't a name you'd call your best friend.

"You got it wrong," Frank started to say. "I'm—"

Mike came running up and grabbed Tom's arm. "Frank and Joe are helping me, Tom," he said. "They're on our side. Let go of him."

Confusion replaced anger on the wrangler's face. Slowly, reluctantly, he lowered his fist and released his grip on Frank's shirt. "Sorry, Frank," Tom said.

"What happened?" Mike asked Frank.

"I was standing watch, and somebody slugged me

from behind, then stampeded the horses," Frank replied breathlessly. "I managed to jump onto Star and bring him back."

"I'll saddle Star and see if I can round up the others," Tom said. "It's likely to be a long job."

"I know," Mike said somberly. "Okay, Tom, get to it. Frank, I'm going to have to go back on our deal and radio for help. With no water and no horses, we can't go on."

He went off to get the CB from the chuck wagon.

Everyone was up and milling around, asking one another what had happened. Word of Mike's decision spread instantly. The whole group seemed upset and disappointed. Even Jessica seemed to have mixed feelings about returning early. Privately, Frank told Joe what had happened to the horses.

Mike came back. "I couldn't raise the ranch," he said. "I'll try again in half an hour."

Jake came over and tugged at Mike's sleeve. "No coffee this morning?" he asked.

"Sorry, old-timer," Mike replied. "We're out of water."

The prospector gave a sly smile. "I told you before, I know where to find water," he said. "Bring some buckets."

"I can't leave camp at a time like this," Mike said. He looked around the group.

"I'll go," Frank said. Nick volunteered, too. Joe decided to keep watch over the camp.

Frank and Nick took two buckets each and followed

Jake down the valley. After five minutes, he clambered into a dry arroyo. They had to pick their way over the large rounded stones that covered the floor of the arroyo.

"You can see here why this valley is called Coyote Canyon," Jake said, pointing toward the ground a few feet away from him.

Frank looked on the ground where the prospector had indicated. There were many paw prints in the dry dust. "Coyotes have been here," Frank murmured.

Nick went over to look. "Must have been a lot of them. Look at all the tracks."

Ahead of them Jake stopped in a spot that looked no different from any other. "This is it," he told them, a glint in his eyes. Frank and Nick approached him.

"It is?" Nick demanded. "Where?"

"I brought you to the place," the old prospector said with a crazy laugh. "Now you do the rest."

Frank was ready to turn back in disgust. Why had Jake pulled such a pointless practical joke? Or *was* it a joke? Frank studied the area more carefully. Most of the plants they had passed had been low, dusty-looking weeds. But at one spot along the side of the arroyo, right next to a big rock, was a bright green bush with red flowers.

"Nick, give me a hand," Frank said. They went over to the bush, and Frank felt the ground. The surface was dry, but when he dug his fingertips under the surface, the soil felt damp. "Let's see if we can move that rock," he added.

They tugged at it. To their surprise, it rolled easily. Behind it was the opening of a low cave, no more than eighteen inches high, with a pool of water at its base.

Jake giggled, obviously pleased with himself. "I reckon Indians dug that, a long time ago. Then everybody forgot it was there. Everybody but old Jake."

Frank dipped out a handful of the water and tasted it. It was cold and sweet. He and Nick used one of the buckets to dip out enough water to fill the other three, then got as much as they could into the one they were using as a dipper.

When they were done, they rolled the rock into place and started back. With every step, the buckets got heavier. Now and then, the water slopped over the rim, wetting Frank's boots. The third time it happened, he stared down at his boots, as if he had just recalled something important.

"Boots," he muttered to himself. "Fancy boots."

Nick overheard him and gave him a wary look.

By the time they reached the camp, Frank's shirt was soaked with sweat. He and Nick gave the buckets of water to Billy Bob, who stared at them in amazement, then started to make a big pot of coffee. As Nick explained to the cook how the water was found, Frank went to his tent to towel off and put on a fresh shirt.

Joe followed him and crouched outside the tent to talk to his brother. "Tom managed to round up three of the horses," he said in a soft voice. "He's off looking for the others now. I checked the area where they'd been tied up. Nothing to show who ran them off, I'm afraid. Any footprints were scuffed away by the stampede."

"That's about what I expected," Frank replied, from inside the tent. After pulling on a T-shirt, Frank clambered out of the tent, and the two brothers stood up, continuing to talk quietly. "But I did some heavy thinking while I was carrying those buckets of water. The most important clue in this case is those punctured jerricans. And they prove just the opposite of what we thought. Here's what came to me—"

He broke off. In the distance, the sound of a car grinding in low gear was followed by angry shouts. Frank and Joe dashed toward the commotion and saw a red-faced Mike standing near a green jeep with the top down. Off-Road Adventures was painted in big letters on the front fender. The jeep was parked off the trail, not far from the chuck wagon.

Joe hurried to the back of the jeep and knelt down to peer at the tires. Then he stood up, caught Frank's eye, and shook his head no.

From the driver's side of the jeep, Roy Ramirez leaned out and said, "I heard you on the CB and figured I'd come by and find out what your problem was."

"As if you didn't know!" Mike shouted. "Come on, 'fess up! You came here to gloat. Well, your plan worked. I'm throwing in the towel. I hope you're satisfied."

"I don't know what you're talking about." The large man opened his door and stepped out. "I—"

Mike had apparently reached his limit. He put his

head down and charged the other man like an enraged bull. Ramirez jumped aside, then faced Mike with clenched fists.

"We've got to stop this," Frank told Joe. He ran forward and got between the two men. "Hold on, you two. Break it up!"

Joe stepped in front of Mike and held his shoulders, while Frank kept Roy Ramirez from getting past him.

From every corner of the campsite, people came running, drawn by the commotion.

"Mike," Frank said over his shoulder, "you've got it wrong. I'm not sure Ramirez had anything to do with all those dirty tricks. I just figured that out two minutes ago."

"Yeah?" Mike retorted. "You reckon you know who did it, then?"

"That's right, I do. And if you'll cool down, I'll tell you *how* I know."

Just then, Tom rode up with two more of the horses. He hitched them to a tree and joined the crowd around Mike, Roy Ramirez, and the Hardys. Billy Bob elbowed his way into the circle, too.

"Mike asked Joe and me to join the tour," Frank explained to the group, "because he suspected somebody was deliberately trying to wreck his operation. He asked us to investigate."

"You mean you're *that* Frank and Joe Hardy?" Nick demanded with awe in his voice. "The detectives? I've read about all your famous cases!"

Frank grinned at him, then continued. "We decided pretty quickly that Mike was right. Teen Trails

West was being sabotaged, but by whom? We were led into more than one blind alley, both accidentally and on purpose."

He stopped to give Jessica a cold glance, and noticed that she looked unusually subdued, even remorseful.

Frank continued. "Then came the night of the three gunshots. By the next morning, Joe and I had four important clues, but it took a while to see what they were and what they meant. We can call them the clue of the flying sniper, the clue of the chilled-out shell, the clue of the rushing water, and the clue of the vanishing slug."

"Wow," Carina exclaimed. "This is just like a mystery story!"

"Shush," Greg said.

Frank caught Joe's eye and gave a slight nod that meant "your turn."

"We searched the area where the sniper had been hiding, first thing the next day," Joe said. "We didn't find a single footprint, or anything to show how he got away after firing those shots. He must have sprouted wings."

"That's number one," Alex said, holding up his index finger. "How about the chilled-out shell?"

Frank said, "It didn't take us more than a minute to run up the hill to the sniper's position, and we found the cartridges from his gun right away. Billy Bob picked one up, and I picked up the other two. All of them were cold."

Tom frowned. "I was right there when you found

them. I don't know why I didn't get suspicious about them," he said. "That soon after being fired, they should have been hot. Warm, anyhow."

"Two," Alex said, continuing to keep score. "What was the next one?"

"A dream," Frank replied. "During the night, after those shots, I had a vivid dream about being next to a rushing river. When I woke up in the morning, I discovered that most of our water supply had been destroyed. When I ran over to the chuck wagon, the ground next to it was still muddy."

"You must have heard the water spilling while you were asleep," Lisa suggested. "That's why you had the dream."

"Maybe," Frank said. "But if the jerricans were punctured during the evening when the shots were fired, why did the water wait until the middle of the night to run out through the holes?"

The group looked puzzled. Then Nick spoke up. "What about the vanishing slug?" he asked. "Does that have anything to do with my centipede?"

Frank laughed. "Not that kind of slug! Joe, would you bring one of the damaged jerricans over here? I should warn you that I'm not one hundred percent sure this will work. So far, it's just a hunch."

When Joe came back, Frank held up the metal can. "Here's the bullet hole," he said, then turned the can around. "Notice that there isn't an exit hole on this side. I saw that yesterday morning, but I didn't realize what it might mean. Now, watch what happens when I pour out what's left of the water."

He unscrewed the cap and turned the can upside down. A little water trickled out.

"Nothing happened," Alex said in a disappointed voice.

"Wait!" Lisa exclaimed. "Where's the bullet?"

"So that's what you meant by the vanishing slug," Nick said. "Okay, I give up. Where did it go?"

Frank glanced over at his brother and saw that Joe had caught on to his theory, even though they hadn't had time to discuss it beforehand.

"The bullet didn't go anywhere," Joe said. "It was never there in the first place. No bullet, and no sniper, either. That's why he didn't leave any tracks."

"But we all heard the three shots!" Jessica exclaimed.

"We all heard what sounded like three shots. My guess is that they were three firecrackers," Frank said, "attached to a single long fuse. The first person on the scene afterward must have collected the scraps from the firecrackers and scattered three spent rifle shells on the ground. The rifle shells weren't hot, because they'd been fired days, or even weeks, earlier. Our flying sniper didn't leave any trail, because he hadn't been up there when we actually heard the shots."

"But Billy Bob was the first one up there," Greg exclaimed. "You mean—!"

Everybody turned to stare at the chuck wagon cook.

"This is nuts," Billy Bob said simply, folding his arms in front of him.

"What about the bullet holes?" Greg asked Frank.

"While everyone else was off on that hike, Billy Bob

must have made those holes with one of his tools—an awl, for instance—then stopped them up temporarily. During the night, when everyone was asleep, he uncorked the holes and let the water drain out. That's the reason the ground was still muddy in the morning. It hadn't been that long since the spill."

"But why?" Mike demanded, turning to face Billy Bob. "Why would you want to ruin me? I never did you any harm. I always paid you well and treated you well. I thought we were friends." Joe noticed that Mike looked as hurt as he was confused.

Billy Bob stared down at his feet. "I don't have to take this," he muttered.

Frank hesitated, then continued. "What we suspect is that he's working with the group that's been looting Anasazi graves in this area. That racket can bring in very big money, with very little risk. But then your operation put a crimp in their plans, Mike. The risk that their grave robbing would be discovered shot up. Their answer was to try and scare you off."

Joe saw that Tom was seething with anger as he looked at Billy Bob.

Under the pressure of so many unfriendly eyes, the cook began to look trapped. He shifted nervously from foot to foot, cleared his throat, and said, "These are all just theories. You don't have a bit of evidence, because I didn't do any of that stuff you say I did. Would I monkey with the brakes on the chuck wagon and take the risk of breaking my own neck?"

"You might," Joe replied, remembering that the cook had been a rodeo rider. "*If* you're someone who's had so much experience jumping off bucking broncos and Brahman bulls that jumping off the seat of a wagon comes easy to you. You had no way of knowing that you'd have me and Nick riding with you."

"More theories," Billy Bob said, stuffing his hands in his jeans pockets. "Guesswork, that's all."

"Not quite," Frank said in a steely voice. "You see, when you slugged me this morning, as I was falling to the ground, I saw your boots!"

Everyone stared at the flashy western boots with the broncos and the three-colored initials. Billy Bob looked down at them, too. Then he sprang forward, knocking Alex down, and jumped into the driver's seat of the ORA jeep. The engine roared. The wheels spun, throwing up streams of dust and pebbles. Everyone jumped out of the way as Billy Bob swung the green jeep around and headed up the draw.

Star was still hitched to a nearby tree. Frank dashed over, jumped onto the saddle, and urged Star into a gallop. As he began his pursuit, Frank heard more hoofbeats behind him and knew it was Joe.

Billy Bob was still in sight. It looked as if he was having trouble finding enough room on the narrow trail for the vehicle. Frank saw him scrape against a big boulder on the right, then veer sharply to the left. His left front wheel bumped up onto a six-inch-high ledge. When it fell off the other side, the undercarriage of the jeep hit the ledge and stuck. The motor screamed in protest. Finally the jeep began to move again, but by then, Frank was even with the left side

145

of the open vehicle. Joe, on his mount, was drawing near on the other side, and Tom was right behind.

Billy Bob saw them and turned the wheel sharply to the left. When Star veered away, Billy Bob swung in the other direction, toward Joe. Instantly Frank freed his boots from the stirrups and used his knees and reins to bring Star as close as possible to the side of the jeep. Then, gathering his strength, he leapt out of the saddle and into the backseat of the vehicle.

He landed sideways on the seat and quickly pushed himself upright. But he immediately was forced to duck as Billy Bob made a blind swing with some kind of metal tool. Frank scrambled behind the cook's seat, grabbed both of Billy Bob's ears, and twisted them hard.

"Hit the brakes," Frank shouted over the man's angry cries. "Right now!"

The jeep came to a shuddering halt in a cloud of dust. Joe and Tom dismounted and hurried over. Joe opened the jeep door, and he and Tom yanked Billy Bob out of the jeep.

"Thanks, guys," Frank said as he climbed out. "We finally caught our trickster."

"Yeah. He was as wily as a coyote, but you handled him just fine," Joe said to his brother. "That was some pretty slick riding, cowboy."

The helicopter from the sheriff's department had just taken off, with a handcuffed Billy Bob aboard. The helicopter had touched down not far from an ancient cliff dwelling, which loomed in the distance. As soon as the dust cloud from its downdraft settled, the whole group gathered around Mike, Tom, Roy, and the Hardys. They all shared a jug of water, each taking a long swallow before passing it on.

"Billy Bob made a full confession," Mike reported to them. "He's the one who dumped the packs off the wagon before we started, and put those pins in the saddle blankets, and all the rest of it. He cut the brake cable and put the hot peppers in the stew. He also did that stunt with the centipede, to make it look like someone was after him. Billy Bob stole Lisa's film, too, because he thought it had evidence against those crooks he was working for."

"The grave robbers, you mean?" Carina asked, in a voice filled with indignation. "What a bunch of slimeballs!"

"I agree," Mike said. "But the great thing is, Billy Bob offered to name the members of the grave looters and to testify against them in court. I can't imagine what made him change his tune so fast."

"While we waited for the sheriff, I had a talk with him," Tom said. "I told him some of the things my people do to those who disturb the sacred sites of Native Americans." Suddenly his solemn face broke into a wide smile. "I made most of them up," he confessed. "But I guess ol' Billy Bob believed me!"

When the laughter died down, Mike said, "I'm glad it's over. I owe a lot to Frank and Joe, more than I know how to repay. But even with the threat gone, I'm not sure if Teen Trails West can carry on. This has been a pretty rough summer, thanks to Billy Bob and his friends."

"I've been meaning to talk to you about that," Roy Ramirez said. "It seems to me that we'd be better off working together, spreading the word about how beautiful this part of the country is, rather than bickering with each other. I don't have anything real solid in mind, but it wouldn't hurt us to talk."

Mike stared at Roy in disbelief. Then a smile crossed his face. "Nope, I reckon it wouldn't, neighbor," he replied. "And I just got an idea that even tops yours."

He reached out, grabbed Jake's sleeve, and pulled him over. "This here," he continued, "is a man who knows the territory better than anyone else alive. If we could convince him to sign on as a guide, I bet we could put something together that no one would beat."

Jake looked momentarily surprised, but then a pleased look crossed his face. "I'm the man for the job," he said eagerly, tipping his hat.

"Now we know who you were talking about when you said someone was trying to kick you off the land," Frank said to Jake.

Jake nodded, and Frank went on. "It was the grave robbers Billy Bob was working for. They didn't want Jake getting too close to their operation."

"Mike?" Jessica said, in a timid voice Frank had never heard before. "I'm really sorry about pulling all those dirty tricks and being such a drip. If I can talk my dad into doing a short film about Teen Trails, you could use it to show people what it's like. I bet you could even get it on TV. And maybe . . . maybe you'd let me come on another tour next year?" The others in the group started to cheer.

Frank turned to his brother and said, "What do you think, Cowboy Joe?"

Joe pushed his hat forward over his eyes and drawled, "Well, pardner, I reckon it's time for us to mosey off into the sunset. Case closed!"

THE HARDY BOYS® SERIES By Franklin W. Dixon

☐ #59: NIGHT OF THE WEREWOLF	70993-3/$3.50	
☐ #60: MYSTERY OF THE SAMURAI		
SWORD	67302-5/$3.99	
☐ #61: THE PENTAGON SPY	67221-5/$3.50	
☐ #62: THE APEMAN'S SECRET	69068-X/$3.50	
☐ #63: THE MUMMY CASE	64289-8/$3.99	
☐ #64: MYSTERY OF SMUGGLERS COVE	66229-5/$3.50	
☐ #65: THE STONE IDOL	69402-2/$3.50	
☐ #66: THE VANISHING THIEVES	63890-4/$3.99	
☐ #67: THE OUTLAW'S SILVER	74229-9/$3.50	
☐ #68: DEADLY CHASE	62477-6/$3.50	
☐ #69: THE FOUR-HEADED DRAGON	65797-6/$3.50	
☐ #70: THE INFINITY CLUE	69154-6/$3.50	
☐ #71: TRACK OF THE ZOMBIE	62623-X/$3.50	
☐ #72: THE VOODOO PLOT	64287-1/$3.99	
☐ #73: THE BILLION DOLLAR		
RANSOM	66228-7/$3.50	
☐ #74: TIC-TAC TERROR	66858-7/$3.50	
☐ #75: TRAPPED AT SEA	64290-1/$3.50	
☐ #76: GAME PLAN FOR DISASTER	72321-9/$3.50	
☐ #77: THE CRIMSON FLAME	64286-3/$3.99	
☐ #78: CAVE IN	69486-3/$3.50	
☐ #79: SKY SABOTAGE	62625-6/$3.50	
☐ #80: THE ROARING RIVER		
MYSTERY	73004-5/$3.50	
☐ #81: THE DEMON'S DEN	62622-1/$3.50	
☐ #82: THE BLACKWING PUZZLE	70472-9/$3.50	
☐ #83: THE SWAMP MONSTER	49727-8/$3.50	
☐ #84: REVENGE OF THE DESERT		
PHANTOM	49729-4/$3.50	
☐ #85: SKYFIRE PUZZLE	67458-7/$3.50	
☐ #86: THE MYSTERY OF THE		
SILVER STAR	64374-6/$3.50	
☐ #87: PROGRAM FOR DESTRUCTION	64895-0/$3.99	
☐ #88: TRICKY BUSINESS	64973-6/$3.99	
☐ #89: THE SKY BLUE FRAME	64974-4/$3.50	

☐ #90: DANGER ON THE DIAMOND	63425-9/$3.99
☐ #91: SHIELD OF FEAR	66308-9/$3.50
☐ #92: THE SHADOW KILLERS	66309-7/$3.99
☐ #93: THE SERPENT'S TOOTH	
MYSTERY	66310-0/$3.50
☐ #94: BREAKDOWN IN AXEBLADE	66311-9/$3.50
☐ #95: DANGER ON THE AIR	66305-4/$3.50
☐ #96: WIPEOUT	66306-2/$3.50
☐ #97: CAST OF CRIMINALS	66307-0/$3.50
☐ #98: SPARK OF SUSPICION	66304-6/$3.50
☐ #99: DUNGEON OF DOOM	69449-9/$3.50
☐ #100: THE SECRET OF ISLAND	
TREASURE	69450-2/$3.50
☐ #101: THE MONEY HUNT	69451-0/$3.50
☐ #102: TERMINAL SHOCK	69288-7/$3.50
☐ #103: THE MILLION-DOLLAR	
NIGHTMARE	69272-0/$3.99
☐ #104: TRICKS OF THE TRADE	69273-9/$3.50
☐ #105: THE SMOKE SCREEN	
MYSTERY	69274-7/$3.99
☐ #106: ATTACK OF THE	
VIDEO VILLIANS	69275-5/$3.99
☐ #107: PANIC ON GULL ISLAND	69276-3/$3.99
☐ #108: FEAR ON WHEELS	69277-1/$3.99
☐ #109: THE PRIME-TIME CRIME	69278-X/$3.50
☐ #110: THE SECRET OF SIGMA SEVEN	72717-6/$3.99
☐ #111: THREE-RING TERROR	73057-6/$3.99
☐ #112: THE DEMOLITION MISSION	73058-4/$3.99
☐ #113: RADICAL MOVES	73060-6/$3.99
☐ #114: THE CASE OF THE	
COUNTERFEIT CRIMINALS	73061-4/$3.99
☐ #115: SABOTAGE AT SPORTS CITY	73062-2/$3.99
☐ #116: ROCK 'N' ROLL RENEGADES	73063-0/$3.99
☐ #117: THE BASEBALL CARD CONSPIRACY	73064-9/$3.99
☐ #118: DANGER IN THE FOURTH DIMENSION	79308-X/$3.99
☐ THE HARDY BOYS GHOST STORIES	69133-3/$3.50

AND DON'T FORGET...NANCY DREW CASEFILES® AVAILABLE FROM PAPERBACK

NANCY DREW® MYSTERY STORIES By Carolyn Keene